PRAISE FOR JAMES SCOTT BELL

A master of the cliffhanger, creating scene after scene of mounting suspense and revelation . . . Heart-whamming.

— **PUBLISHERS WEEKLY**

A master of suspense.

— **LIBRARY JOURNAL**

One of the best writers out there, bar none.

— **IN THE LIBRARY REVIEW**

There'll be no sleeping till after the story is over.

— **JOHN GILSTRAP**, NYT BESTSELLING AUTHOR

James Scott Bell's series is as sharp as a switchblade.

— **MEG GARDINER**, EDGAR AWARD WINNING AUTHOR

One of the top authors in the crowded suspense genre.

— **SHELDON SIEGEL**, NYT BESTSELLING AUTHOR

ROMEO'S STAND

A Mike Romeo Thriller

JAMES SCOTT BELL

Compendium Press

Compendium Press
Woodland Hills, CA

Neutral men are the devil's allies.

— EDWIN HUBBEL CHAPIN

I think we need a gunslinger, somebody tough to
tame this town.

— JOHN FOGERTY "GUNSLINGER"

ROMEO'S STAND

We were an hour from Las Vegas when the plane began to shake.

It was a few weeks before the word *pandemic* became ubiquitous on our collective lips and America closed up shop with a massive case of the heebie-jeebies. The people on the plane were blithely breathing each other's air and coughing into their fists. The tourists and players in Vegas were bumping shoulders and sharing dice at the craps tables, unaware that their favorite playground would soon be as empty as a politician's promise.

Karen, the nice woman seated next to me on the plane, gripped her armrests.

"Just a little turbulence," I said.

She gave me one of those tight smiles that work hard to hide anxiety.

"Sure," she said.

"Happens over the desert," I said. "Hot air. Like a lawyer in court."

My attempt at humor was as shaky as the plane. Karen lost the smile as the plane shudders intensified.

Then we dropped for two full seconds. Which, for most people, seems like two minutes out of a disaster movie.

Passengers screamed.

Karen sucked in a labored breath, closed her eyes.

Instinctively, I put my hand on hers.

"It'll be all right," I said.

She opened her eyes, looked at me. The plane dipped again and she let out a yelp.

"Hang in there," I said.

Another drop.

More screams.

Then a vibration, as if the plane was suddenly atop a giant washing machine on spin cycle.

"What's happening?" a woman yelled.

The speaker alert sound bonged, followed by a voice. "Ladies and gentlemen, this is the captain. Don't become alarmed. We are going to be making an emergency landing. We will easily make it to a small airport just ahead, so try to stay calm and by all means stay seated with your seat belt fastened. This will all be—"

The plane shook hard, dropped again.

People screamed like they were on a roller coaster.

The little boy in the seat behind me started crying.

Karen pressed the back of her head against her seat.

"Ladies and gentlemen," the captain said, "listen carefully, and stay calm."

Another drop. More screams.

"Put your feet flat on the floor, hug your knees, and put your head in your lap."

Karen looked at me, eyes wide.

"Feet flat," I said.

She positioned her feet on the floor.

"Head down and hug those knees," I said.

She hesitated. I gently slid my hand behind her back and helped her into the position.

"We'll be fine," I said, and sounded like I believed it.

K ansas City, MO, was where we were coming from. I was out there to interview a witness for one of Ira's trials. Ira Rosen—former Mossad, now rabbi and lawyer in Los Angeles—is my only real friend. That is if you don't count Carter "C Dog" Weeks, a beach kid who hangs around me at Paradise Cove. I've been trying to keep him off drugs and train him in the rudiments of a productive life. He seemed to be taking to it. I actually missed him while I was gone.

The witness in KC, Ken Raney, was a graphic artist who used to work in LA and, while he was there, saw a guy running away from the scene of an attempted armed robbery. The robbery happened at a Subway sandwich shop on the first floor of the historic Bradbury Building downtown. The guy Ken Raney saw bore a slight resemblance to our client, Lester Wiley. Wiley was nabbed two blocks away, based on a description given by two of the employees. The robber had worn a bandana—cowboy outlaw-style—wielded a gun, then got freaked and ran.

Lester Wiley didn't have a bandana on him, but he did have a gun. That's bad, but attempted armed robbery is worse. Ira and I didn't believe Lester was the robber. Ken Raney was one of four eyewitnesses and he believed the perp was not our client.

The interview went well, though Raney did not want to testify if there was a trial. I took his sworn statement. Ira wanted to get the attempted robbery charge dropped. With no priors on his sheet, Lester would have a good chance to be charged only with a misdemeanor and maybe get summary probation.

The gun the robber flashed was described with slight differences by the Subway employees. That's the hard truth about eyewitnesses. In the heat of the moment, with all that adrenaline, it's common for each wit to "see" different things.

But in this case, two of the descriptions of the gun were similar enough to make it unlikely that Lester's gun was the one used in the robbery. Or at least, it would make the prosecution's burden of proof on the matter difficult. That's a card we had to play, so I was off to interview Dr. Cary Bukowski, PhD in Criminology and former firearms instructor at Quantico, who could appear at the trial as an expert witness in firearms.

Just a short flight to Las Vegas.

Until it wasn't.

When I first got on the plane, Karen was in the window seat reading a paperback. I had the aisle and she gave me a brief, welcoming smile before going back to her book. She was forty or so with light brown hair, dressed in tasteful casual. I was happy she had a book. It meant I could read, too, in relative peace. I'd brought an old paperback I'd taken from Ira's shelf, one I'd been meaning to read for a long time— *Zen and the Art of Motorcycle Maintenance: An Inquiry into Values.*

We took off fine. Everybody seemed relaxed. A couple of guys in turned-around baseball caps were already greased for Vegas. I'd seen them drinking at the airport bar, watching the big-screen TV showing a football game. I pegged them as college boys, probably Mizzou, the Italian-pasta-dish nickname for University of Missouri.

Across the aisle, an older couple occupied the two seats. They looked comfortably married, like they knew each other's preferences and moods without saying a word. I wondered what it would be like to have someone like that in my life. But then again, if I did, would we even make it to middle age? My life the last couple of years seemed to make it only a 50/50 proposition for me.

When we were about half an hour into the flight I noticed my row companion tearing off the cover—I think I saw *Patterson* on it—and some pages. She folded the discarded leaves and stuck them in the seat pocket in front of her.

To each her own. I went back to my book.

Fifteen minutes later, she did it again.

"Excuse me," I said. "I couldn't help noticing your reading method."

She smiled. "I get these at yard sales for when I travel. I don't want to carry the whole book around with me."

"Unique," I said.

"My mother did the same thing," she said. "I guess I picked up the habit."

"Well, no one can say you don't give a rip about reading."

"Ha ha."

"I'll be here all week. My name's Mike, by the way."

"Karen."

"Nice to meet you, Karen."

"What's that you're reading?"

I showed her the book.

"What a title," she said.

"It was pretty popular in its day," I said. "So I've heard."

"Sounds philosophical."

"It is," I said.

"You like that sort of thing?"

"I do."

"Is that why there's Latin on your arm?"

"Very good," I said.

"Something about truth over everything?"

"Truth conquers all things," I said.

"Ah," she said, and got a faraway look. "It'd be nice to believe that."

"We have to," I said. "Or we're sunk."

"Do you mind if I ask what you do?" she said.

"I'm sort of a freelance investigator for a lawyer in Los Angeles."

"Sort of?"

"There's no official job description." I didn't tell her I'd had to kill a few people and break the bones of many others. After all, we'd just met.

"How about yourself?" I said.

"Oh, not that interesting."

"I don't believe that."

"How could you know?"

"We're all pieces in the big jigsaw puzzle, right? If one piece is missing, we don't get the whole picture. Everybody is interesting in some way. Of course, interesting doesn't always mean legit."

Her expression got intense. I wondered if I'd stepped in something. But she didn't look like the non-legit kind of puzzle piece to me.

"I didn't mean to pry," I said.

"Oh, no," she said. "I was just thinking how different life in L.A. must be, compared to Wichita."

"That's true about every place that isn't L.A," I said.

"You do have the weather," she said.

"But you have . . ."

She laughed. "Museums and humidity."

"Two very underrated things," I said.

"Humidity is underrated?"

"Saves you money on joining a spa."

We went back to our books. She tore off more pages, giving me a puckish sideward glance.

I immersed myself in one of the "Chautauquas" that form the philosophical content of *Zen and the Art of Motorcycle Maintenance*. And came to a stunning passage:

> The purpose of scientific method is to select a single truth from among many hypothetical truths. That, more than anything else, is what science is all about. But historically science has done exactly the opposite. Through multiplication upon multiplication of facts, information, theories and hypotheses, it is science itself that is leading mankind from single absolute truths to multiple, indeterminate, relative ones.

Which means, of course, that if truth conquers all things—like I've got tatted on my arm—science isn't the last word. Or even the most important.

And as I was contemplating yet again what the way might be, the plane started going down.

Forty minutes later neither one of us was reading.

W e didn't hit any runway in some little airport. What we hit was the ground with a bone-rattling slam and grind. It sounded like a cement mixer dragged over a parking lot. My seat belt dug into my stomach and my chin bounced off my chest. Good thing my tongue was resting easily inside my mouth or there would have been blood.

From there we skidded and bumped some more then stopped with a suddenness that must have jarred some heads at the cervical-vertebrae connection. For a brief moment we had silence, as if everybody was taking a breath. Like when you first wake up from a bad dream and you wonder if it really happened. Only this time, it really did.

And then came the sounds, crying and wailing, the boy behind me screaming.

Karen was bent over, as instructed.

But she wasn't moving.

"You all right?" I said, putting my hand on her arm.

No answer.

I put my hand on her forehead and lifted her slightly so I could check her breathing. I unbuckled her seat belt and raised the armrest between us. I unbuckled myself and got up so I could turn her and lay her down on the seats. I pulled her legs up at the knees and got her feet planted on her seat so blood would flow to her head. I patted her cheek and said her name.

Her eyes fluttered. Then opened.

"It's okay now," I said. "Are you hurt?"

"I ... don't know."

"Just rest. Help will be coming."

I looked out the window and saw only blanched, hot desert and wondered what kind of help could get to us. How far were we from a town? How could vehicles get out here? They'd have to be off-road types. Maybe choppers for the severely injured, if any.

The intercom crackled.

"Ladies and gentlemen, please stay in your seats. We are assessing the situation. There is no danger."

"My husband is hurt!" a woman shouted. "Help!"

The boy kept screaming.

"Shut that kid up!" a man yelled.

A woman's voice answered, "You shut up!"

A dozen other voices talked over each other. A harried

flight attendant, her face scrunched up, tried to make her way down the aisle, but four or five people were standing in her way. She attempted to get them to sit back down but only two did.

The intercom again. "Please keep in your seats, ladies and gentlemen. We are calling for help, and if you stay calm you will be attended—"

"I want to get out!" a man shouted. "I want out of this plane!"

Other voices raised up in agreement.

The flight attendant argued with a man who refused to sit down.

"I hurt," Karen said.

"Where?" I said.

She pointed to her ribs.

"Lie as still as you can," I said. "Breathe easy."

But I realized breathing was not going to be easy. For anybody. Because the plane was getting hot inside. No air circulating. We were a big metal tube on the desert floor in the middle of the afternoon.

Intercom: "We need to know who is injured. Please help us identify the injured by staying in your seats and raising your hand. Please do that now."

I started to put my hand up.

"Don't bother," Karen said. "I'm not that bad."

Over the next several minutes two things happened. The flight attendants assessed the personal injuries, and the plane got hotter.

Many of the people were on their phones. One man shouted, "I need to make a call! Why can't I make a call?"

A girl of fifteen or so was videoing the scene with her phone. Plane crash coming soon to you via Instagram.

"It's hot," Karen said.

"Let us out!" a woman yelled.

I kept thinking of frying pans and fire.

The captain came back on and said they'd begin taking people off, but to bring any covering we had, like hats and sunscreen. They would be erecting temporary shelters. There was water for everyone, he said, but don't drink too much, too fast.

"Can you help me out?" Karen said.

"Might be better for you to stay put," I said.

"I'm a little claustrophobic," she said. "Sorry."

"I'll see what I can do."

"Mike?"

"Yes?"

"Thank you."

"Do you have sunglasses?"

"In my purse. Under the seat."

I got her purse.

"In a blue case," she said.

I found the case and got the sunglasses. My backpack was under the seat in front of mine and I got my own shades. Then I helped her sit up.

"Pain?" I said.

She shook her head.

By this time they'd opened the rear door of the plane. I got Karen to her feet. The flight attendant with the furrowed brow—or, I should say, the more furrowed of the two attendants—put her hand up to me.

"She's shaken up and needs air," I said.

"There's an evacuation slide," the flight attendant said. "Please take your seat cushions for shade."

Karen held my arm as we lined up. I took the slide first so I could help her as she came down. We each had our cushions and I'd snagged a blanket off a shelf in the back bay. Once outside I spread the blanket near the tail and had Karen sit on it.

"Okay?" I said. I held one cushion over her head and another over mine.

Karen said, "Breathing better. A little woozy."

"Nice, steady breaths," I said. "Can you hold this?"

She nodded and took her seat cushion in both hands.

"I'll be right back," I said. I put my cushion on the blanket and went to the rear door. The mother and son who had been behind me got on the evacuation slide. The boy sat on his mother's lap. He had a smile on his face. The mother did not. They held their seat cushions to their chests.

When they got to the ground I helped the mother up. The boy said, "Can we do it again?"

The furrowed-brow flight attendant helped an older man onto the slide.

"Can you send down some water?" I said. "I'll distribute."

She nodded once and sent the old man down with his cushion. When he reached the bottom I gave him my hand. His grip was pretty good.

"Fine thing," he said as he walked away.

"I'm going to give you a tray of waters," the flight attendant said. A moment later she slid one down. It held a couple dozen small plastic bottles.

I went back to Karen and handed her one. "Sip slowly," I said.

Around us it was starting to look like an encampment. As instructed, people were using their seat cushions not to float on the sea but to keep the sun from frying their faces.

Some people were in various stages of shock or panic. I picked the faces with the most worried looks and gave them a water.

One of the two guys in the backward baseball hats came to me with his hand outstretched. I pulled the tray away. "Kids and old people first," I said.

"Gimme a water," he said.

"I'll be back."

He gave me a two-word response and moved to grab a bottle. I caught him by the wrist.

"Don't make a scene," I said.

"Let go," he said. "You want me to kick your—"

Before he could inform me what part of my body he was going to kick, I bent his arm, twisted him around, forced him to his knees.

"We're all hot enough out here," I said. "Don't make things hotter."

I let him go and finished handing out the water. I got several *Thank you*s, two *God bless you*s, but not another *I'm going to kick your* ...

Civil society was being restored.

K aren was holding steady, sipping her water.

"You want me to call your husband?" I said.

She snapped a surprise look at me.

"Your wedding ring," I said. "Am I presuming?"

"No," she said.

"He'll expect to hear you landed safely in Vegas."

"I'll call him myself. I'm still a little shaky."

"Still have a pain inside?"

She took a breath and winced. Nodded.

"Do you have any idea where we are?" she said.

"I'm guessing about two hours from Las Vegas by highway. Two days if we have to go by pack mule."

"Thanks for trying to lighten things up," she said.

The male flight attendant had his coat off and was under

the wing holding a clipboard. I went over to him and said, "The woman sitting next to me, seat 36A, may have a concussion and maybe something internal."

He looked at the clipboard.

"Her first name is Karen," I said.

The flight attendant ran his finger down the list. "Morrison."

"She's sitting down by the tail."

"Is she somewhat stable?"

"For now," I said.

"We're expecting transport to Dillard. There's a critical access hospital there." He looked around. "Dear God."

I gave him a pat on the shoulder and went back to Karen.

About twenty minutes went by before the first off-road vehicles started to show up. Citizens from the town, it looked like. Made my heart glad. A desert Dunkirk. Strangers helping strangers simply because they were in trouble.

"It won't be long now," I said to Karen.

"I wish I had my purse," she said.

"You shall have it," I said.

I went to the evacuation slide and did my best running-up-the-down-escalator trick. Made it like an American ninja.

The plane was almost empty now. I went to Karen's seat and saw her purse under the seat in front. Some of the contents had spilled out. I pushed it all back in. Then I grabbed my backpack and turned and noticed a middle-aged guy in a shirt and tie, just sitting there, blank-eyed.

"This just doesn't happen," he said to no one in particular.

"Time to get off," I said.

He stared. "Just doesn't happen."

I took his arm and helped him up.

"What are you doing?" he said.

"Let me help you."

"Let go!" He jerked his arm away.

"It's all right," I said.

"Don't tell me that. Nothing is all right!"

It sounded like he was talking about life. I wasn't going to argue the point. I left him for the crew to deal with and slid out of the plane.

When I got back to Karen a guy of about twenty-five, good shape, wearing a clean black T-shirt and jeans, was helping her to her feet. I got on the other side of her and held her arm.

"This way," the guy said and led us to a silver Ram Power Wagon. At least I think it was silver under the coating of dust and dirt.

"You'll take her to the hospital?" I said.

"Yep," he said.

He opened the passenger door and we helped Karen get in. I handed her the purse, closed the door.

Through the open window she said, "What will you do?"

"I'm going to stay here awhile," I said. "If I don't see you again, take care."

She smiled and extended her hand. I took it. She held on for an instant longer than what was normal for two parting strangers. She looked at me with eyes that reflected a momentary sadness. Even a longing.

Or maybe it was just my imagination.

Then the truck growled and pulled away.

· · ·

Next came the helicopters. One military chopper landed far enough away so it didn't kick too much sand in our faces. Two military personnel, complete with aviator sunglasses, emerged and jogged over to the scene. They were met by our pilot who was gesticulating wildly. A picture of calm he was not.

Then another helicopter showed up, this one with a big 13 on the side. The news. It began a slow circle over the distressed citizens below.

A dark-skinned young man with a pronounced Indian accent and wearing a knit shirt with PARAMEDIC on the back asked how I was.

"Aces," I said.

"Sure?" he said.

"I'm fine."

"If you'll come this way, a vehicle will transfer you to Dillard."

"I can wait," I said.

I followed the paramedic around as he tended to some folks. We got an older man who was woozy into a Jeep. Then we got a young mother and her eight-year-old daughter on a 4x4 Mitsubishi.

No one was put on the military chopper, which was a good sign.

The news eggbeater headed off in the direction of the departing off-roaders. The action was shifting to the town.

Now I was ready to get out of there. I wanted to check on Karen Morrison, then head off to Vegas for a quick, professional interview.

Then I could go home.

Um, no.

. . .

A bearded old coot offered me a ride. He wore blue jeans with red suspenders and a faded flannel shirt taut against a beach-ball belly.

"Sure," I said.

"Hop in," he said, motioning to a red, two-seater dune buggy.

I got in and put my backpack on my lap.

"Most exciting thing that's happened out here since Mary Louise Edgerton sat on a gila monster," the coot said.

"Ouch."

He settled himself in the driver's seat. "You got that right. Stuck his teeth into her right buttock and that was almost that. Luckily, Mary Louise is tough as a fifty-cent steak. She was back up and tending her chickens in a day. Let's ride."

He fired up the buggy and off we went.

"My name's Mike," I said.

"Harrison," he said. "Folks call me Moochie. I sort of look like him, don't I?"

"Who?"

"Moochie! You know ... ah, you're a young man, you don't know who Moochie was. On an old TV show back in the day."

He proceeded to tell me about a child actor named Kevin Corcoran and his character on a TV serial called *Spin and Marty*. He said he and Corcoran were the same age—though the actor had died back in 2015—and he, the Moochie who was driving me, bore a striking resemblance to Corcoran and that had earned him the nickname Moochie in elementary school.

After ten minutes more of hearing all things Moochie, we came to a thin strip of sandy road.

"Smooth as a baby's behind now," Moochie said.

I think he was referring to the road we were bumping along. Smooth is in the eye of the driver.

Then I saw the town of Dillard rising in the desert like a potted cactus. Out here there is nothing but scorched earth blanketing both sides of an asphalt vein that connects little outposts like this to the beating heart of Las Vegas. The blanched, squat buildings were sugar cubes in the afternoon sun, with two gas station signs trying mightily to provide a skyline for the baking burg. New York has nothing to worry about.

"Not much," Moochie said, "but I call it home.

We pulled into a dirt lot next to a Quonset hut from the year 1948 or so. A bunch of other vehicles used in the rescue effort were there, too. Passengers were being directed into the hut by a couple of state troopers.

"This is where they want you," Moochie said.

"Where's the hospital?" I said.

"Two blocks that a-way," he said, pointing. "And one block to the left. You can walk to it. Heck, you can walk to anything in Dillard."

"Thanks for the lift."

"Maybe you can join me later at Biff's. I'd be happy to buy you a beer."

"Biff's?"

"Finest tavern this side of Vegas."

"Are there any other taverns this side of Vegas?"

"Not that I can think of," he said. "Come on by. I like talking to you."

"Sorry, Moochie, but I'll be trying to get to Vegas right away."

"Shame." He stuck out his hand. I shook it.

"Don't sit on any gila monsters," he said.

"Lesson learned," I said.

I got out and went toward the Quonset hut. One of the troopers, holding a clipboard, asked my name. I gave it to him.

He checked the clipboard, made a check mark with a pencil. "If you'll go inside, please."

"How long's this going to take?" I said.

"As fast as we can, sir."

"I need to get to Vegas."

"If you'll just go inside," he said.

"On your manifest," I said. "A woman named Karen Morrison was seated next to me."

"Please, sir."

"I'd like to make sure she's okay."

"Are you going to be a problem?" the trooper said.

"Probably," I said.

He inhaled and stood upright. I inhaled and stood still. It was a real picture of male bonding.

Looking back at his clipboard he said, "She has not come through me. Maybe someone inside can help you."

From the signage on the walls I got the impression that this was an American Legion meeting hall. There was red, white and blue bunting wrapped around wooden brace beams. Two long tables took up the length of the hall, with plenty of chairs.

I recognized many of the passengers, who were in various stages of distress, anxiety, and no doubt some PTSD. A humming, like the sound of a moderately noisy factory, filled the place.

A stout woman in a crisp white shirt and dark pants was standing at one end of the hall handing people cups of water. The epaulets on her shirt were a sure sign of Salvation Army.

I didn't mind that at all. The Salvation Army does a lot of good. Except for the bass drum, of course. But no drums were in sight.

A young woman in professional dress, looking rather thin and nervous, spotted me standing there and came to me. She also had a clipboard.

"You are a passenger?" she said.

"Was," I said.

"Of course. May I have your name?"

"Mike Romeo."

She looked at her clipboard. "Yes, yes, I see." She looked back at me. "Are you injured in any way?"

"Not in any way that matters," I said.

"Do you have a headache, nausea, anything like that?"

"Nothing like that," I said.

"Would you mind if I gave you a nystagmus test?"

"Watch the birdie?"

"Just this pen," she said, and held it up to eye level. "Keep your head steady and follow the pen." She slowly moved the pen to the left then back to the right.

"Good," she said.

"Will I be able to play the violin again?" I said.

"What?"

"Old joke."

She didn't smile.

"May I have your phone number?" she said.

"Are you a lawyer?" I said.

"Does it show?"

"I work for a lawyer," I said. "This makes me naturally suspicious."

"I'm just collecting information," she said.

"Are you local?"

"If you'll—"

"Is this town big enough to support a lawyer?"

"Please—"

"If I was really suspicious, I'd say you were fishing for clients. But from the looks of things, what with the plane still cooking out in the desert and you already with the passenger manifest, you must be doing preliminary legwork for the airline."

She said nothing.

I said, "Probably the biggest thing to happen around here since Mary Louise Edgerton sat on a gila monster."

"Excuse me?"

"You missed that?"

"Missed what?"

"Mary Louise ... Look, I am not hurt and I'm not going to sue anybody. I just want to get to Vegas."

"As a service, our firm is arranging transportation for those well enough to travel. But we strongly recommend a medical examination here in town before a decision is made."

"I've decided. When can I get a ride?"

"Soon."

"I'll be back."

It was mid-afternoon outside. I started walking toward where Moochie said the hospital was. I passed a branch office of the Nevada State Bank in a bleached cake box of a building, and a store next to it painted a garish orange. The sign said *Whitey's Bookstore.* The bookstore looked more secure than the bank. It had some plastic chairs outside under a wooden awning. The center of the town's intellectual life, no doubt.

Further on was a hardware store that bore an ACE logo,

a Pace gas station and Biff's Watering Hole. Biff's looked like the kind of watering hole they'd have in Dillard. Think more hole than water.

Then I saw it. Dillard Regional Hospital. A faux-adobe building with a Spanish tile roof. It had three skinny palm trees in front of the entrance, going for the oasis look. There was a lot of activity out front, people going in and out, cars and two emergency vehicles pulling into the parking lot.

The waiting area inside had half a dozen people or so in various attitudes, some waiting, some asking questions at the front desk. I joined the latter group. Two middle-aged women in light blue smocks were handling the phones, the questions, and the computer monitors. The one on the left finished with a guy in a cowboy hat, then turned to me.

"Yes?" she said.

"I'm here to check on Karen Morrison?"

"Are you family?"

"I was on the plane with her," I said.

"We're very busy as you can imagine."

"I'd just like to know how she's doing."

"That isn't possible at the m—" She cut herself off and reached for the phone. She swiveled in her chair so her side was to me.

I have an advanced degree in body language. Translated, she was saying, *Don't bother me, please. Why don't you walk over to the DQ and order yourself a chocolate shake?*

Instead, I walked down the corridor like a lab rat looking for the cheese. I poked my head inside some double doors, which led to another corridor and some noise. A Latina in scrubs almost hit me coming out.

"Excuse me," she said. "You can't be in here."

"I'm looking for someone."

"This is emergency."

"She's from the plane that went down," I said.

"Everybody's from the plane that went down," she said.

"Please," I said. "Karen Morrison. How can I find out?"

She thought a moment, then said, "If you'll just go and wait near the front, I'll see what I can do."

"That would be great. Thanks."

I went back to reception and sat on a white vinyl sofa by the doors. I took out my phone and called Ira Rosen.

"You in Vegas?" Ira said.

"There's been a delay," I said.

"You're still at the airport?"

"I don't think they have an airport here," I said. "Except maybe one of those little ones that brings in mail."

"What?"

"Our plane went down in the desert."

"What?"

"Plane. Down. Emergency landing."

"Heavens!"

"Yes, I'm all right. Thanks for checking."

"Michael, where are you?"

"A place called Dillard."

"Dillard," Ira said and I could tell he was hitting the keyboard. "Hold on a second. Here we go. Dillard. Let's see. According to the 2010 census, population 3,657. Elevation 6,047 feet. Old silver mining town. Stopover for tourists on the way to Vegas. There's a Shoshone reservation nearby. This is interesting. A military testing site to the south is the main source of employment."

"What are they testing?" I said.

"The F-117 Nighthawk. Oh my ..."

"What?"

"Don't drink the water," Ira said.

"Terrific."

"When are you getting out of there?"

"They're supposed to be getting me a ride to Vegas."

"Where are you now?"

"I'm in a small hospital. Right now it's more like one big emergency room. They're looking at some of the passengers."

"But you're okay?"

"I was sitting next to a woman, and I'm trying to find out how she is."

"Is that necessary?" Ira said.

"Isn't there some Chinese proverb about being responsible for somebody you help out of danger?"

"You're not Chinese, Michael."

"But I dig Confucius."

"So what are you trying to accomplish?"

"I just want to see if she's okay. She has a family back in Kansas. Maybe I can help get word to them."

"Do you know her name?"

"Karen Morrison."

"Common name," Ira said. "What's her approximate age?"

"Forty."

"Hold on," Ira said.

I held on and looked over at the receptionist I'd talked to earlier. She was giving me the stink eye. I smiled and nodded. Her eye kept stinking my way. A couple of medics walked by the desk heading to another part of the facility. The receptionist motioned to one of them. He went to her and she whispered something in his ear.

Ira came back on. "I don't think I can be much help here. If you can get me more information, I can limit the results."

"Our witness in Vegas, can he wait?"

"He lives there."

"Maybe you can call him and tell him I've been delayed."

"How long do you think you'll be?"

"I hope not too long."

"That's vague," Ira said.

"Life is like that sometimes," I said.

A man in a white short-sleeve shirt, black pants, and slip-on black shoes approached me. He was about forty-five, almond-colored skin, and black hair slicked down with some industrial-strength mousse.

"Excuse me," he said. "You were asking about someone who was brought in?"

"That's right, Karen Morrison."

"You can understand that we have a lot going on here and can't be giving out information at the current time."

"And you are?"

"I'm one of the administrators."

"What would be the best way for me to find out what happened to her?"

"May I ask what your connection is with this woman?"

"I was on the plane next to her when it went down. I helped her. I just wanted to follow up and see if she's okay. Make sure her family hears about her."

"Believe me, we will notify all family at the proper time."

"What about notifying me?" I said.

"I'm sorry. I hope you understand, at this time ..."

"That doesn't seem very sporting," I said.

"Excuse me?"

"It's odd."

The guy gave me a long, steady look. "Is there anything else I can do for you?"

"What was the first thing?" I said.

He didn't reply.

I didn't pursue.

But something smelled. And it wasn't disinfectant.

I decided to test my nose at Biff's. Which smelled like beer, old eggs, gym socks, and Yucca trees. It was done up western-style, with a big skull of a longhorn steer over a pool table. There was a long bar, at the end of which sat Moochie.

"Hey!" he said, raising his hand. "Change your mind about the beer?"

"I believe I have," I said and took the stool next to him. I set my backpack on the ground.

"That all you're carrying?" Moochie said.

"I travel light," I said.

"Clean underwear and a toothbrush," Moochie said with a nod. "Man doesn't need much more."

The bartender, an older guy with the build of a Dickens undertaker, was talking on a landline phone. He said something, hung up, came over and said, "Have?"

"Dos Equis," I said.

"Out," he said.

"You have the sign." It hung over the only window in the place.

"It's a good sign. You want a Tecate?"

"Sure," I said.

Moochie said, "Glad you could stay awhile."

"I hope it's not awhile."

"Now that's no way to talk. This is an okay place. If you like small-town life. Do you like small-town life?"

"Never tried it."

"Where do you hang your hat?"

"I have a little unit near the beach in LA."

"Oh, that place gives me the heebies and the jeebies and

everything in between. You got to be crazy to live out there."

"I am a little crazy. Aren't we all?"

The bartender put a glass, unfrosted, and a can of Tecate in front of me. At least he opened the can.

"Can't argue with that," Moochie said. "No sir. There's a little crazy in everybody. I guess that's what you've got to watch out for. You got to keep the most crazy out of the way, and let the normal crazy people do their own thing."

"That's a fine, Platonic view of government."

"A what with the what, now?"

"Plato. He wrote a book called *The Republic*."

"Oh yeah, Plato. He was a Greek, right?"

"One of the smart ones."

"Those Greek guys didn't have much to do but walk around being smart, did they?"

"If you weren't a slave or a woman," I said, "and you had money or a patron."

"You some kind of college professor or something?"

"Far from it." I filled the glass with beer.

"You look like you could hold your own in a fight."

"The only thing I like to hold is the occasional beer," I said, hoisting my glass. I took a drink. He laughed and took a swig of his own.

I said, "You know the people around here pretty well?"

"I should. Been here a long time. Almost twenty years now."

"You know the folks who run the hospital?"

He gave me a squint, suspicion squeezing his eyes. "I might."

"Just asking," I said. "I talked with a dark-haired guy, slicked back."

"Maybe you mean Gus Deveroes."

"If I did mean Gus Deveroes, what can you tell me about him?"

Moochie put his glass down. "I don't run in his circles."

"How many circles do you have out here?"

"Two. There's towners and frowners. Towners are the folks who live here and accept their lot in life with a smile on their face. And there's those who live here but don't want to be here, and kind of look down on those of us who do. Gus is a fellow who always seems to be walking around with that attitude. I've only talked to him three or four times in the last five years, which is when he came here. Didn't get much out of him, except that he's the kind of guy who needs a lifetime supply of Pepto-Bismol."

"Does he have a reputation?"

"With the ladies?"

"With the money."

"Not sure what you mean."

"He administers a hospital. There's got to be money out here. Does he seem on the up-and-up?"

"To be honest, I haven't thought about it. I've only been in that place a couple of times, for surface stuff. They take Medicare. Lot of us old-timers go there."

"How about the lawyers in town?" I said.

"We got ourselves a three-person firm," Moochie said.

"I think I met one of them," I said. "She was gathering info at the Quonset hut."

"She? Must be Sally Hoskin then."

"Why's that?"

"Because the other two are men," Moochie said. He elbowed me gently in the ribs and lowered his voice. "I'm old school. I still think you can tell the men from the ladies."

Just then sunlight streamed into the bar. The front door

had opened. And a twirling baton came in. Attached to the baton was a woman.

I could tell.

She was dressed in a one-piece, red-white-and-blue spangled bathing suit. With white, knee-high boots. She was working the heck out of that baton. She could have been a high school cheerleader, except she was at least fifty years old.

"That's Candy Sumner," Moochie said. "She's a regular. Puts on a routine and somebody buys her a drink. If you play your cards right, you might get yourself a private show." He nudged me again with his elbow.

"Not my kind of card game," I said.

"Me either," Moochie said. "I went from 'why not' to 'why bother' years ago."

Candy Sumner tossed the baton into the air. It hit the ceiling. She caught it and resumed her routine. She went around her back, through her legs and finished with a flourish, if bending at the waist and spreading your arms can be considered a flourish.

She got scattered applause from the patrons.

Smiling, she came to the bar and sat to my left.

"Hello, stranger," she said. "Buy a girl a drink?"

"Beer?" I said.

"I was thinking of something more adult. Jett, Seven and Seven."

The bartender started making her drink.

Moochie said, "This is Mike. He came out of that crash."

"No fooling?" she said. "You look like you came out fine."

She looked me up and down.

"Mind if I ask you a question?" I said.

The bartender set her drink in front of her. She picked it up, smiled, and said, "I'm all ears, lamb chop."

Then she downed half her drink.

"You've lived here awhile," I said.

"He wants to know about Gus Deveroes," Moochie said, a little too loudly.

"Ha!" Candy Sumner said. "Don't turn your back on him."

"Now, now," Moochie said.

"Why would you say that?" I asked.

"I can tell about people," Candy said. "I got an eye."

"You got two," Moochie said.

Candy said, "You know what I think?"

"No," I said. "What?"

"There's a reason and a season for everything, and the two come together only once or twice in a person's life."

She smiled at me.

"I got a feeling," she said, "you might be the one to bring 'em together for me."

"Cut it out, Candy," Moochie said.

"What do you think?" she said.

I said, "How'd you come up with this theory?"

Before she could answer, a country-boy-looking guy— long hair, cowboy shirt, boots—appeared on Candy's other side.

"Come on over and I'll buy you another drink," the guy said.

Candy didn't even look at him and said, "I'm fine right here. Jett, hit me again."

The country boy put his hand up to the bartender and said, "She's gonna drink that with me."

"Leave me alone," Candy said.

"Oh boy," Moochie said.

I said, "I'm having a conversation with Ms. Sumner."

The country boy said, "I'm not talking to you."

I turned to Moochie. "Is this the local barroom brawler?"

"Forget him," Moochie said.

"But he's impolite," I said.

"What did you say?" Country Boy stepped away from the bar top and took a step toward me.

I spun around on the stool. "It's too hot for unpleasantness. Civil discourse is what's called for here. How about I complete my conversation with Ms. Sumner and then she can, if she so desires, join you at your table?"

"How about I shut your face?"

"What part of civil discourse did you not understand?"

"Get up," he said.

"Don't," Candy said. "Just don't. I'll go."

"You don't have to," I said.

"Yes, I do." She picked her baton off the bar and started toward a table by the door. Country Boy gave me a side glance as he followed her.

"Better this way," Moochie said.

"I feel like I'm in a bad Western."

"Better a bad Western than a good chick flick, I always say."

"Who was that?"

"Till Felton. One of those guys you always want to stay clear of."

I drained my beer and reached for my wallet.

"Let me take care of it," Moochie said. "You're a guest. You may never come back."

"I'm wondering when I'm going to leave."

"Huh?"

"Not until I get some answers."

Moochie stroked his beard, leaned forward and spoke softly. "You some kind of law?"

"Only the law of unintended consequences."

He shook his head. "You have the funniest way of talkin'. I just thought ..."

"What did you think?"

"Maybe you were here to clean up this town. Like Audie Murphy."

"There's an obscure reference."

"My old man loved Audie Murphy."

"And you're waiting for one to come along?"

Moochie shrugged. "I'm just saying there's cleaning up that needs doing, is all. And if I thought you were the law, I'd say I'm here to help."

"Thanks for the beer," I said.

"Don't be a stranger," he said.

I f there is a place, besides a bar, where you can get some answers about a small town, it would have to be a bookstore. Owners of such places operate on low margins and high intelligence. They read, so know human nature through the great literary conversation. They also sell, so know human nature through the avenue of commerce.

The only question was getting them to talk. I decided to take the soft approach and stopped at the bargain bin set up outside the store. It was full of paperbacks and had a sign that said *50¢ each, 5 for $2*. It was an eclectic mix of romance novels, thrillers, mysteries, along with one of the Patrick O'Neal sea epics, a book on homeopathic medicine, *The Hite Report on Male Sexuality*, and a one-volume history of the United States that looked like it was published around 1965. I snatched that out of the bin. I could brush up on my knowledge of the French and Indian War while waiting for the proprietor.

A moment later a robust middle-aged woman, gray of hair and dressed in a red tank top and blue jeans, came out and gave me a smile.

"Afternoon," she said.

"Howdy," I said. I can speak local lingo with the best of them.

"Passing through?"

"I was on the plane."

Her face shifted to concern. "Oh my gosh, are you all right?"

"I'm looking for a good book," I said.

"Doctor my eyes! What was it like?"

"Like?"

"Being on the plane, crashing like that."

"It wasn't really a crash," I said.

"But the pilot."

"What about the pilot?"

"You don't know?"

"Apparently not."

"He died."

"The pilot died?"

"One of them," she said. "Heart attack." She shook her head. "Life."

"Indeed," I said. "Did they get him to the hospital?"

"I don't know about that," she said.

"My name's Mike." I extended my hand.

She seemed surprised by that, but took it. "Ginnie Peacock," she said.

"Live here long?"

"Twenty years."

"The hospital here, is it pretty good?"

She shrugged. "As they go, I guess. Why?"

"There was a woman sitting next to me on the plane. I want to make sure she's all right."

"You just go up the street that way about—"

"I've been there. They just didn't give me any information."

"Oh."

"I was talking about it over at Biff's, with Moochie."

Ginnie Peacock smiled. "Old Moochie."

"Yeah, and Candy Sumner."

"Ugh."

"And a guy named Till Felton."

"Doctor my eyes, but you get around fast—" She stopped herself as her demeanor changed. A frosty glaze of skepticism crept into her eyes.

"You're military police, aren't you?" she said.

"No."

"The way you're asking questions."

"I'm just a guy from the plane."

Nodding skeptically, she said, "See anything you like?"

"Oh," I said. "Yeah. Maybe this one—" I held up the U.S. history book, and reached for the O'Neal— "and this one."

"One dollar," she said.

"A bargain," I said.

"Which is why they're in the bargain bin," Ginnie Peacock said.

"I'm sharp that way," I said.

I fished in my wallet for a buck, handed it to her.

She nodded curtly.

I said, "If I were military police, would you have reason to be suspicious of me?"

"That's a trick question," she said.

"It is," I said. "I will level with you, Ms. Peacock. I work for a lawyer and was on my way to Vegas to interview a witness. My stop here has nothing to do with it. I was sitting next to a woman on the plane and when I went to the hospital to check on her, I was sort of given a runaround."

I studied Ginnie Peacock's face. It remained impassive.

I said, "So if I were to ask you about the hospital, is there anything you could tell me?"

For a long moment she looked straight at me. Then said, "We're a small community here. And you're a stranger."

"I'm also a customer," I said.

"You're welcome to buy more books. I'll be inside."

T here's a great old movie called *Bad Day at Black Rock.* Spencer Tracy stars as a stranger who gets off a train in a small desert town. He starts asking questions, and the people there get very suspicious, very fast. Because they're hiding a secret.

So I was feeling a little like Spencer Tracy as I walked back to the hospital. Military police? What was buried around here?

When I entered the reception area the same reception-ist I'd dealt with before motioned to me.

"You were asking about a patient," she said.

"Karen Morrison," I said.

She put a pad and pen on the counter. "If you could give me your contact information, we'll get in touch when we know something."

"You don't know anything now?" I said.

"All I was told was to tell you that," she said. "And also that a driver has been arranged to take you to Las Vegas."

"And who arranged that?" I said.

"I don't know that, sir."

"Sally Hoskin?"

"Sir, if you'd like to wait over there, a driver will be with you shortly."

What a tidy little hospital. They didn't give you any information readily available to them, but they did give you a driver to whisk you out of town.

I started toward the door.

"Sir."

I kept walking.

O utside the sun was still a hot orange ball in the clouds to the west.

What was I doing?

Small town, small hospital, they're not going to have instant tabs on all passengers. And sure they'd be a little put off by a nosy stranger. Why was I looking to stick around and make trouble?

There was a witness waiting for me in Vegas. I, therefore, had a professional duty to attend to, and should get right to it.

But there are other duties. Some are imposed upon you. Others you create for yourself.

Why Karen Morrison? Why now?

Maybe because philosophy teaches us we have holes inside us, and our task is to fill them, find the answers. Unless you're an existentialist and don't believe in answers, only questions. Then you die and your grave marker says *All dressed up and nowhere to go.*

But some of us have to keep looking, and every now and then that hunger is transferred over to the other part of your life. And right now my hunger was telling me someone was hiding the truth, and if my forearm tattoo means anything, it means I don't like people trying to hide the truth. Truth has a hard enough time as it is.

Cars and trucks and the occasional emergency vehicle were still buzzing around the hospital. I'd already seen the sights and sounds down the main drag, so I walked the other way toward the sign in the distance: *Three Rivers Motel.*

One river would be enough for me.

Closer, I could see the front of the place had three neon signs: *Arcade. Bingo. Hot Slots.* As I walked in the front doors I heard dings and whirrings and video game noises.

Behind the front desk was a skinny guy in a black vest and bolo tie. He was looking at his phone.

I stood there for a second.

He looked up.

"Welcome to Three Rivers," he said.

"I'd like a room with a view of the rivers," I said.

The gaunt face did not crack a smile. "Single room?"

"Yes."

He tapped a keyboard and looked at a monitor. "We have a king, forty dollars, includes tax and fees."

"Do I get unlimited use of the rivers?" I said.

Frowning, he said, "There are no rivers here, sir."

"I just thought, you know, the sign and all."

"Would you like the room?"

"What does it have a view of?"

"The parking lot."

"Aces," I said. "Just what I came to this part of the country to see."

Still no smile. "May I see some ID?"

"I'll pay cash," I said.

"I, um, I still need to see some ID."

"Why?"

"In order to take your credit card."

"I'm not using a credit card."

"For incidentals."

"I don't use incidentals. I have an aversion to incidentals."

He looked confused, so I took out two twenties and a ten. I put the twenties on the desk and held the ten out to him.

He didn't look confused anymore. He took the ten and folded it and put it in his pocket.

"I just need a name," he said.

"Phil Rizzuto," I said. "With two Zs."

He tapped the keyboard, then coded a key and put it in a sleeve. He wrote 108 on the sleeve and handed it to me.

"There's a continental breakfast in the morning, Mr. Rizzuto," he said. "Café, casino and arcade open all night." He pointed. "Around that corner and to your right."

In the café I sat at the counter and ordered an egg salad sandwich and glass of milk. I munched and listened to the dingings and bleeps and whirlies of the various arcade games and video slot machines. The sound of brains softening and bodies atrophying. I'm a cheery fellow when I'm tired and hungry.

N ow all I wanted was some sleep. But my neighbors in Room 110 were having a party, and the night was young.

I called Ira.

"I'm going to spend the night here," I said.

"Why?" Ira said.

"I'm going to try to find out where Karen Morrison is."

"It sounds like you're having a good time."

"Next door. I'm in a motel."

"How are you getting to Vegas?"

"They have all sorts of people handing out rides," I said.

"Don't take too long. Mr. Spooner is expecting you at two."

"I should be there."

"Should?"

"Sorry, Ira, gotta go. I've got a party to go to."

I knocked on the door to 110. No answer. I felt the door vibrating from the music.

I knocked again, louder.

The door flew open, the handle in the hand of a woman laughing about something that just happened inside. In her other hand was a champagne flute, half full.

"You're late!" she said.

"I am?"

"Come in!" She held the door open with her foot and grabbed my shirt and pulled me inside.

"I'm next door," I said.

"That's great!" she said. "Come on!"

Her exuberance was clearly oiled with the bubbles of sparkling wine.

"Hey! He's here!"

A round of cheers went up from the gathered revelers. The sound of the cheers sounded exclusively female.

And, indeed, that's what awaited me. The room, a suite, was filled with women. They were in various positions, from sitting to standing to leaning, and all had some form of drink in their hand. On a round table by a credenza was a spread consisting of cheeses, grapes, bottles of wine, and two large bottles of Jack Daniels.

"Turn it down," my hostess ordered. A second later the music came to a stop.

"What do you think?" she said to the throng.

A chorus of positive sounds issued from the assemblage.

Uh-oh.

I said, "There's been a mistake."

The hostess said, "I don't think so!" and motioned with her arm. That drew a big cheer.

Then to me she said, "If this is a mistake, I'll take ten. You are so much better than I imagined."

"I'm just passing through," I said. "I'm in the next room. And I—"

"We can always move the party in there," she said, and bobbed her eyebrows.

Someone shouted, "Tell him to start taking it off!"

Another said, "Yeah, start the show!"

Still another: "Get him a drink!"

"All I want to know is how long you're planning—"

Someone shoved a champagne flute in my hand.

"Is he going to strip or not?" a voice shouted.

"I vote for not," I said.

Various protests came.

"We can make it worth your while," the hostess said. "How much?"

"I'm flattered," I said, "but—"

"At least take off your shirt," she said.

A chant started up: *Shirt, shirt, shirt, shirt!*

A couple of hands pulled at my shirt.

I said, "Ladies, please, this is not 1990."

A woman in a tight red dress—said tightness not unappealing—pushed her way toward me and announced, "Let me take care of this." She immediately took my arm and started me toward the door.

"Hey!" the hostess shouted. "I saw him first!"

"Chill out," the woman on my arm said.

Various verbal protests were uttered, but then the door opened and I was in the hall with this woman in the red dress, holding a glass of sparkling wine, hoping what happened in Dillard stayed in Dillard.

"Come on," she said.

She led me to the exit doors at the end of the hall. A security guard came in. Young, roly-poly, florid of face. He gave us a nod and held the door open for us.

"Thanks, sergeant," the woman said.

Then we were outside in the warm night.

"I knew you wanted to get out of there," she said.

"Thanks," I said, and raised the champagne. "Just to be sociable." I drank a bit.

She took the glass from me and drained it. Smiled. It was a nice smile, not gaudy. Would have been down-home but for the makeup, which seemed a little excessive. Her dirty blonde hair was of the earth. Her big round eyes were of the moment.

"My name's Heather," she said.

"Phil," I said.

She tossed the champagne flute into the bushes. "Do you have any weed on you?"

"I'm afraid not."

"Too bad," she said.

"What's going on in your room?"

"Birthday party for one of us. You were supposed to be the stripper."

"Life is funny that way," I said.

"The night's not over," she said.

I cleared my throat.

"We're from Oklahoma City," she said. "We're on our way to Vegas."

"Like everybody else here," I said.

"We're writers. We have a little group."

"Oh? What do you write?"

"Erotica," she said.

"Shocking," I said.

She laughed. "I have a series out on Kindle, about OKC firemen. It's called Red Hot Hoses."

I tried to think of something to say.

Heather said, "How would you like to be the cover model for my next book?"

"Gee, as much as I'd like—"

"What *do* you do?" she said.

"I'm just a tourist," I said, and as I did I sensed something behind me.

I turned just in time to see a chain whizzing toward my head.

T he ability to move from low alert to high alert in a fraction of a second is a skill that must be practiced. Once it is in the muscle memory of the brain, it becomes something like instinct.

The Marines call this being "left of bang." Think of an attack—a gunshot, an IED, a fist to the face—on a timeline. There's a before, then the *bang*, then the after.

On the timeline, to the left of bang is where you have to train to be aware.

Most people go through life without any awareness at all. Driving, walking, shopping, it's all la-dee-dah. Until *bang*. They are not even on the timeline until it's too late.

Marines are trained to have a level of awareness consistent with the circumstances. At the very least, you should be assessing your surroundings, taking in data, looking for signs. Eventually, that becomes second nature.

When you pull together all the data—which is happening fast in the synapses of the brain—and conclude there is a possible threat, you move your focus closer to the bang. You're still left of it, but ready if it comes. And if lethal force is going to be necessary, you're ready for that, too.

But you have to train your brain for this. Virtually all people, when faced with imminent danger, either freeze up or run for their lives. Their first move isn't to fight back.

Mine is.

So even standing outside in the desert air, I was on auto-alert to movements around me. And when I turned and saw the chain coming my way I did not freeze. That mechanism has been disabled.

I ducked and dove.

The chain whistled over my head as I drove my shoulder into the attacker's gut. At the same time I grabbed his legs at the knees and yanked them off the ground.

Down he went, his head making a satisfying thunk on the flagstone walkway.

I pushed off him, yanked the chain out of his hand, spun around behind his head and wrapped the chain around his neck. He was now a dog in Romeo's Obedience School.

The whole thing took about six seconds.

Something squeaked, like a mouse running for its life.

It came from Heather's throat. Her mouth was open, her eyes wide.

"Go find the security guard," I said.

She didn't move. Her mouth stayed open.

"Now, please," I said.

"That ... that ..."

"Please," I said.

She nodded and raced back into the motel.

The guy with the chain was Till Felton, the jerk from Biff's.

I pulled him by the chain up to a sitting position.

"What's this about?" I said.

His mouth opened a little but nothing came out.

I tightened the chain. His mouth open a little more.

"Somebody put you up to this," I said. "Not even a dipstick like you would come out over a little thing that happened in a bar. I'm going to loosen the chain so you can breathe and you're going to tell me who you're doing this for."

I let the chain go a little. He gasped for breath. And then he managed to utter a couple of unfriendly words.

So I taught him some more obedience.

He made a coughing, gurgling sound.

I loosened again and said, "Well?"

He shook his head slightly.

I used the end of the chain to give him a thunk on the head.

He screamed, as much out of surprise as pain.

"Who sent you?"

"No ... body."

"You just decided to track me down on your own?"

He nodded.

I popped his head again with the chain.

"Ow! Come on!"

"Why?"

"You were ... trying to score with Candy."

"Please," I said, and gave his melon one more plunk.

He screamed and cursed and shouted, "Stop doing that!"

"Stop what?" I said. "This?" I clanged him again.

Now he growled like a chained animal, which is what he was. He jerked around and grabbed at the chain around his neck. I held it tight.

"You going to talk to me?" I said.

He nodded. I let him have some air.

"This isn't about Candy Sumner," I said.

"Don't hit me, man!"

A voice said, "Let him go."

It came from just outside the door. It was the round security guard. And he was holding a stun gun.

Heather was right behind him.

"He started it," she said to the guard. "The guy with the chain around his neck."

"Sir," Security said, "let the man go."

"Not until the law gets here," I said.

Security blinked a couple of times.

"So here's what you do," I said. "Call the sheriff's office. Tell them I'm holding a guy for assault with a deadly weapon and to send a deputy."

"I didn't do nothin'!" Felton said. "This guy's trying to kill me!"

"He's lying!" Heather said.

"I'm in charge here," Security said.

"Just make the call," I said.

"Not until you release him," Security said.

"If I do that," I said, "he's going to take off."

Security took a step toward me, and showed me the stun gun. "I'm asking you for the last time."

Now I was annoyed. Keeping hold of the chain, I took a step and kicked the stun gun out of Security's hand.

"Get it," I said to Heather.

When Security started to move I grabbed a handful of his white shirt and held him.

"That's mine!" Security said.

"You'll get it back," I said.

Heather had the stun gun now and held it like it was a bomb about to go off.

"You're in big trouble, man," Security said.

"Make the call." I pushed him toward the door.

He tried to look like he still had swagger as he went in. I

felt a little sorry for the guy. When a security guard loses his strut, he's got precious little dignity left.

Felton said, "Just lemme up, man. This ain't right."

"You feel like talking?" I said.

"I already told you."

To Heather I said, "How'd you like to test that thing?"

"Me?"

"Sure."

"What ... do I do?"

"Give him a jolt in the neck."

"No!" Felton said.

"I don't think I can do it," Heather said.

"You're a writer, right?"

"Yes."

"Consider this research. Someday you'll write a book—"

"Don't do it!" Felton said.

"—about a guy who just won't learn manners—"

"Come on!" Felton said.

"—and has to be taught the hard way." I winked at her. She caught on. "I like it," she said.

"Don't!" Felton said.

A woman from the party room came out the door, holding a drink.

"What's going on, Heather?" she said.

"Look at this," Heather said, showing her the stun gun. "And that." She waved toward me and my chained prisoner.

"Whoa," the woman said. "Bondage?"

"You're drunk," Heather said.

"I can see. I gotta tell everybody!"

"Don't," I said.

But she was already heading back into the motel.

. . .

The great standoff ended when a local sheriff's vehicle pulled into the back lot of the motel. By that time what looked like the entire OKC erotica group was outside, holding drinks, talking, laughing, taking phone pictures. One was scribbling in a notebook.

The roly-poly security guard was there, too, looking as wide-eyed as an English explorer trapped on the Island of the Amazons.

The deputy who emerged from the cruiser was middle-aged and had a pronounced western shamble. Not exactly John Wayne, though he looked like he was trying.

"All right," he said, "what goes on here? Is that Till Felton?"

Felton said, "This guy's crazy!"

I have to admit, holding the chain around Felton's throat did not look normal.

Security said, "I tried to get him to let him go."

The deputy looked at me. "Let him go."

I said, "This churl attacked me with this chain."

"This what?" the deputy said.

"Chain."

"No, the other word."

"Churl?"

"What's that supposed to mean?"

"A churl is a disagreeable and ill-educated fellow," I said.

"Let him go."

"Only if you arrest him for assault," I said.

Heather was now next to me. "I saw the whole thing. He did it. He tried to kill him!"

"Who are you?" the deputy said.

"My name is Heather Hawks."

"The writer," I said.

One of the other writers called out, "That's right!"

"Let him go," the deputy said, and put his hand on the butt of his sidearm.

"This is on you," I said. I let go of the chain.

Felton got up, rubbing his neck. "He tried to kill me, Sam!"

"Does he look dead to you?" I said.

Sam the Deputy said, "Let's go down to the station."

"I don't think so," I said.

"You can't do that," Heather said.

Deputy Sam pointed at her. "Stay out of this."

I said, "You're telling a witness to stay out of the thing she witnessed?"

Deputy Sam took a step back from me and drew his sidearm.

"Really?" I said.

"In the car, sir."

"You going to shoot me in front of all these people?"

Several pairs of female eyes lasered in on the representative of the law.

Now Deputy Sam didn't look quite so confident.

"Tell you what," I said. "Drop this whole thing and I won't swear out a complaint against Mr. Felton here."

A few of the OKC writers murmured affirmatively. One said, "We will all testify!"

"Amen!" said another.

Deputy Sam looked confused, maybe a little intimidated. A man in that condition, wearing a gun and the imprimatur of the law, has two ways to go. He can double down, or find a way to back off without losing face.

The deputy chose door number two. Without holstering his weapon he said, "All right. Why don't we all just call it a night, huh? Everybody back inside. Till, you come along with me."

Till Felton rubbed his neck and gave me one of those looks an owned guy flashes when he's got nothing else.

I rattled the chain at him.

"I'll take that," Deputy Sam said.

I gave it to him. "Make sure I don't see this, or Mr. Felton, again."

"Have a good night," he said.

"Oh, he will," Heather said.

Deputy Sam and Felton started to the sheriff's car.

I took the stun gun from Heather and handed it to the security guard. "All's well that ends well," I said.

"Whatever," he said.

"You did fine."

"You disarmed me."

"That's good," I said, putting a hand on his shoulder. "Now you know. Never take that thing out unless you're up close, and intend to use it. It's no good as a threat. Now go have a Coke."

I started back toward the motel.

Followed by the erotica writers of Oklahoma City.

I t was like a paparazzi mob scene. Phone cameras outstretched. Excited voices. One woman asked me if she could write my story, another if she could interview me, another if she could do further research on me in my room. Heather asked if I'd be interested in coming to Oklahoma City to speak at their annual conference.

And they were not so subtly moving me back toward 110.

My plan to stay under the radar in Dillard, Nevada, was not going well.

I said, "Thanks for the support, but I'd just like to get some sleep now."

"Not gonna happen," a woman said.

Heather stepped in front of me and faced the others. "Come on, guys. Let's let him get some peace and quiet." To me she said, "I'll hold them off. Go on."

"Thanks," I said.

Some departing cheers sent me on my way. I got back to my room and plopped into a chair in the darkness.

I'm not surprised at the low estate of humanity, as evidenced by a local thug who wanted to take my head off with a chain. Philosophy and theology are in agreement that male nature is a disaster waiting to happen. It needs restraint, self-reflection. Because those are often lacking, we have laws.

But that doesn't stop canker sores like Till Felton from infecting our societal gums.

Jesus once said, "The poor you will always have with you."

If I'd heard him say that, I probably would have added, "The punks, too."

I was sure Felton wasn't acting alone. Somebody put him up to it. It wasn't over Candy, either. It had something to do with the hospital, and my inquiries about Karen Morrison.

Why would that be an issue for anybody in a little town like Dillard?

The party was going again in 110. This time it didn't bother me. They'd come to my support. Let them have a good time.

I could always read until my brain told my eyes to close. I turned on a light and fished out the U.S. history book from my backpack. I thumbed through it and landed on a page with a passage the previous owner had highlighted. The chapter heading was "Westward Expansion."

But there was also the ideal of individualism. This democratic society was a mobile mass of freely circulating atoms, each seeking its own place and finding play for its own powers and for its own original initiative. We cannot lay too much stress upon this point, for it was at the very heart of the whole American movement. The world was to be made a better world by the example of a democracy in which there was freedom of the individual.

I chewed on that a moment, sitting in a motel on a plot of ground in the west, where a lot of "freely circulating atoms" were throwing dice at craps tables, doubling down at blackjack, and feeding slot machines, if not coming after people with chains.

Was this the ultimate outcome of rugged individualism? Was this the American dream?

And then I was dreaming myself. It was one of those doesn't-make-any-sense dreams that was either trying to reveal deep layers of psychological trauma, or was just the dyspeptic fusion of egg salad, milk, and champagne in my stomach. In the dream a pack of pink mice were chewing at my feet as I held a bottle of Windex. Before I could ask any of the rodents a question, I was awakened by a pounding on the door.

The digital clock read 2:39. The party next door was apparently over.

Another knock, more insistent. I got up and went to the peephole, half expecting to see one of the literary set from the great state of Oklahoma.

It was another uniform. Or half uniform. The guy was about five-four. Sam the Deputy towered behind him.

I opened the door.

"Come on, man," I said. "I was sleeping."

The little sheriff—for that is what he turned out to be—

had a weathered, middle-aged face over a weightlifter's body.

"We need to talk," he said.

"Why?" I said.

"I'm the sheriff, Les Cullen. Mind if we come in?"

"I haven't done a thing to the place," I said.

"This shouldn't take long," Cullen said.

You never want to hear that from the law.

We sat down like old friends.

Cullen had steel-wool hair cut short. It was thick, though, and when he ran his fingers through it, it looked like it wasn't without a fight.

"Mind if I ask your name?" Cullen said.

"I don't mind if you ask," I said.

"I'm asking."

"I don't mind."

Cullen cast an impatient look at Deputy Sam, then said, "You gave your name to the desk as Phil Rizzuto."

"It's a good name," I said.

"Yeah, the old Yankee player. Who are you really?"

"I'm a private citizen, which means I like privacy."

"You're about to be arrested, chum. No privacy then."

"What for?"

"I have cause to hold you for assault," Cullen said. "Based on what Sam has told me."

"I thought we called this off," I said to the deputy. He shrugged.

To Cullen I said, "Did Sam tell you I have a witness who saw the whole thing?"

"The girl?"

"I believe she's a woman," I said.

"Got the hots for you, does she?"

"The hots? Did you really just say *hots*?"

Cullen said, "A biased witness don't fly around here."

"That'd be for a judge or jury to decide," I said.

"It doesn't have to go that far. But you do."

"What, you're telling me to get out of town? Like in a movie?"

"Or I could take you down to the calaboose and let you cool your heels for a couple of days. Then you can flap your gums at a judge. But you'll get charged and there'll be bail, and all that. You want that?"

"Why the muscle?" I said. "What makes me so special?"

Cullen half-smiled but said nothing.

"Have something to do with the hospital?" I said. "Something about me asking questions about a woman who was on the plane? Maybe the hospital doesn't like it. Maybe Gus Deveroes doesn't like it."

Shaking his head, Cullen said, "Nah, we're a friendly town."

"That's so clear to me now."

"And my friendly advice is, pack up, and Sam here will do you a service and drive you to Vegas."

"How about we all sleep on it?" I said. "And tomorrow I'll get up, take a shower, have some breakfast, and give you a call."

Cullen stood. "Not going to work for us. Let's go."

There's a time to fight, a time to stand down, and a time to keep your lips zipped. I was having a hard time deciding, over the next two minutes, what it was going to be.

If I fought, I'd only bring down more trouble on my head. Which meant trouble for Ira, trouble for the case I was working on. From Las Vegas I could regroup. Talk to Ira. Figure out a way to get information on Karen Morrison in some legal fashion.

Or maybe I should just forget about her. Was she really my concern after all? No, that wasn't the issue. I knew this was about me, my stubbornness, my refusal to give up on something once I sink my teeth into it.

Maybe I was part gila monster.

So I went along. I didn't give Cullen or Deputy Sam any more lip, either.

It was only when I figured out I was going to be killed that I decided to say something.

When Deputy Sam pulled off the highway and onto a dirt road, I said, "Don't do it."

"Do what?" Sam said.

I was in the back seat talking to him through the grated partition.

"You won't be able to keep it a secret," I said.

"We're taking a shortcut to avoid a holdup," he said.

"At this hour?"

Only the hum of the engine answered me.

"You ever kill anybody, Sam?"

Nothing.

"I have," I said. "It messes you up. I mean, for good. You're going to have nights when you wake up in a cold sweat, when you feel like barfing for no reason, when—"

"Shut up!"

"You see that? See what it's doing to you already?"

"I said shut up!"

"Or else what?" I said.

Silence.

"You have to think things through, Sam. You've only thought one step ahead. But you're going to have to live in steps three, four, five and forever."

We bumped along, the night enfolding us.

"Maybe before you off me, Sam, you can tell me what's going on. Why all this? What did I happen into?"

He started to slow.

"Come on, Sam, it'll be good for your soul. Oh, did you think about that? Your soul?"

More bumping.

I said, "Aristotle said that to attain any sure knowledge about the soul is one of the most difficult things in the world. Does the soul exist on its own? Or must it always be joined to a body? If a soul exists apart from the body, where is it before the body is formed? Or is it created upon conception? Who, then, does the creating?"

Nothing from Sam, but he looked stiff.

"Lucretius thought the soul was material. You know, you can touch it. What do you think, Sam?"

He didn't answer.

"What happens to the soul when we die? Is there a judgment? Is there a heaven and a hell?"

These were darn good questions. I'd have to give them more thought, and soon.

The car skidded to a stop. He popped open the door and got out.

A second later the door to my left opened and a flashlight beam hit my face.

"Out," Sam said.

"Descartes tended to equate soul with mind, or understanding. Do you understand what you're doing, Sam?"

"I'm pointing a gun at you," he said.

"You want to blow my soul all over the car? There's blood involved, you know."

In the short pause that followed I could see, in my mind's eye, the confused face of a young deputy who'd gotten himself too deep into something. At least I hoped that was the case.

"You don't get it," he said. "I'm not going to shoot you."

"You drove me here for a chat?"

"I'll tell you where you can go," he said. "If you promise never to come back."

"And you'd believe me?" I said.

"Come on, man. Get out."

I made a quick triangle assessment of the space between Deputy Sam, the squad car door, and the rear of the vehicle. As I put my left foot on the ground I knew he was standing too far away for me to make an effective lunge.

Once I was all the way out, he said, "Turn around and start back toward me."

"That's an odd request for someone about to let me go," I said. "Are you sure about this?"

"Now!"

"Truth is confirmed by inspection and delay, falsehood by haste and uncertainty."

"What?"

"Tacitus."

I have found, under similar circumstances, that the well-dropped name from ancient literature causes just enough delay in the synapses of an antagonist to allow for one, quick movement.

Which I made.

Pushing off to the left and lowering my head, I made it behind the squad car when the first shots were fired. I was out of the light beam for a second as I took off into the darkness.

And zigged.

The beam found me.

More shots.

I zagged.

Three more shots and the pinging sound of ammo hitting hard rock.

He had to be about out of bullets and would have to change out the mag. But he'd also have to choose to follow me with the light or not. And whether his soft body could keep up with me wasn't a concern. As long as I didn't trip on a freaking rock in the night, or run head on into a cactus. At least I was wearing Adidas running shoes. Did they make desert shoes? I'd have to find out if I survived.

I juked to the right. Then the flashlight beam found me again and *blam*—

I went down.

Once, I was flattened in the cage by a bruiser who called himself Chato. It was one of those unofficial tournaments in Kentucky. He clocked me with a right to the side of the cranium, the hardest punch I've ever taken in my life. Like a bag of auto parts dropped from a roof, I hit the mat, jangling and loose and almost out. Chato hopped on me and gave me two more bricks to the head before the ref stopped it.

A day later, in the hospital, I got a visit from a hanger-on named Beckwith, a small guy who was always on the make for a fast buck. He told me he had some information for me that would interest me, but it would cost a C note. I almost ripped the IV out of my arm so I could introduce it to Beckwith's backside. He must have seen my eyes because he said he'd defer the C note until after I verified the information, and from there it was my discretion.

He then proceeded to tell me that Chato had put Plaster of Paris powder on his hand wraps. That's an old trick. Under the gloves your sweat hardens the powder and boom, you've got loaded gloves.

That's what my head felt like now. Like Chato—who I found later and called Cheato before I laid him out with an elbow to the face—had clocked me again.

On the desert floor now, I rolled on my back and felt

the side of my head. It was wet. Blood was pouring but wasn't gushing.

Small consolation as I saw the beam of light heading my way.

I somehow got up and ran. I even did the serpentine thing. Must have looked like a zombie running the last mile of a marathon.

I looked back. The beam was trying to follow me.

But no more shots.

I could turn and try to take him out. But I was dizzy and he'd be quick to reload.

The only way was to get out of range, out of the light's reach.

With all the strength I had left I told my legs to keep running. My legs answered that they'd do their best, but what about your bleeding head? We can discuss that later, I told them, then hit a rock with my foot.

I stumbled and down I went again.

And heard something growling in the distance.

An animal?

No. A motorcycle?

With unsure steps and dizziness starting in on me, I wobbled into the uncertain gloom. But now, up ahead, I made out something big and dark. A formation of some kind.

Rocks.

Big rocks.

A place to hide out if that motorcycle came looking for me.

My head was throbbing. Blood leaking out of me. What chance did I have out here?

And it would get cold soon, maybe very cold. I only had on a Hawaiian shirt and khaki shorts. The rocks up ahead would have retained some heat from the day. That could be some small comfort. My sedimentary Motel 6.

I got to the rocks and indeed it was a substantial outcropping. There was enough starlight to see that it was at least ten feet high, though I couldn't tell how thick it was. I needed to get on top so I had a view.

Weak and slimy was how I felt now. My right hand was sticky with blood as I'd been using it for a fleshy bandage. I stopped and listened for a moment. Remember that old song about the sound of silence? Well, it was on full blast.

Had they given up the search?

What about tomorrow?

I was able to feel my way up about four feet. The rocks were warm. But I couldn't see where to take my next steps, or find a place to grab. I had no idea where cracks or crevices might be.

But I had nothing else to do. Why not a little rock climbing as long as I was conscious?

If I'd had a phone I could call Ira or Vegas cops or something. But I only carry a secure burner and that was in my backpack, which was in Deputy Sam's car.

Fine. He was welcome to my underwear and a phone he couldn't use.

I did have my wallet, which was a great comfort. I had all the cash I'd need to buy food from the caravan of taco trucks that were sure to roll by.

U sing my hands like a blind man, which wasn't such a stretch at the moment, I felt for grabbing areas and ledges. My plan, such as it was, was to find a place where I could lie down flat for awhile. I had no idea what my plan would be after that.

One step at a time, right?

Which is what I did, up the rocks.

And got to something like the top of the outcropping.

King of the hill. I allowed myself a moment to savor a moment's victory. I knew it would be my last for awhile.

But if I could make it through the night maybe I could swing another small victory in the morning. As in trying not to get found by the bad guys.

From here I could see the lights of Dillard in the distance.

Completely uninspiring.

In the other direction, much further away, some lights that were perhaps from the military base.

Slowly, I slid along the top of the rocks to get a look at the other side. I'd have to find some sort of cover in case I passed out. Up here would be like a frying pan if I made it to tomorrow afternoon. I didn't want to go out as Mike Romeo, skillet steak.

I slipped.

My left leg went straight down.

And pulled me along with it.

Then I stopped with the suddenness of a rear-end collision.

Because I was wedged.

Torquemada could not have designed a more efficient torture. My left leg was as stuck as a driven nail. I had no leverage to push myself up. My arms were too low against the faces of the rocks. My right leg was bent at the knee and useless for anything.

Well now, Romeo, what was it Ollie used to tell Stan? *Here's another nice mess you've gotten me into.*

That was my brain trying to be funny. Because I knew I

could very well be facing a long, slow death by dehydration if I didn't get out of there.

But I couldn't get out of there. I tried nuance of movement to dislodge the leg. It would not dislodge. Slowly it began to dawn on me that this rock formation would be my sedimentary cemetery—the final resting place of Mike Romeo.

I've been close to death before, but it was always sudden. This time it was going to be a long, slow slide across the River Styx. My mind, I discovered then, had a mind of its own. A big part of it was observing me, curious as to how I'd react. Looking for some sort of meaning in all this, my brain became a flurry of flash cards tracing the history of thought, from Plato to Camus, looking for someone or something in philosophy to latch on to.

Augustine.

Averroes.

Aquinas.

Pascal.

Descartes.

Give me something, boys.

The Vedas.

Upanishads.

Dharma.

Buddha.

Noble truths. Life is suffering.

Stars, world, pain, rocks, night. All swirled, became one, merged into a white blackness of dreams...

...and I was in Times Square, holding my mom's hand, walking toward the subway. My head throbbed and my shoulders were filled with fire. Every step sent a tiny explosion through my bones. Somehow I knew I was eight years old.

"Are you all right?" my mom said.

"I hurt," I said. "I hurt all over."

"Why do you hurt?" she said.

"Because people are mean," I said. "They're trying to kill me."

"Silly, who would want to kill you?"

"Them," I said, looking at all the faces in Times Square, going this way and that, but every face looking at me, unsmiling.

"You're safe with me," my mom said, then I tripped and fell on my face on the sidewalk. I started to cry. I wanted my mom to pick me up.

But she didn't.

I got to my knees, calling *Mom!* through my tears.

She wasn't there.

I screamed for her.

The people kept walking past me, wordless, glaring, then there were more of them and they came into me in a crush, pushing at me. Clawing at me.

And then it was dark, and silent, and I wasn't eight anymore.

I smelled dirt and rock.

I was back, but how long had I been here?

And where was here anyway?

I was alive.

I was going to stay alive, somehow.

We owe God a death, I thought, remembering what Feeble says in Henry IV, Part 2. *And he that dies this year is quit for the next.* But I wasn't ready to pay my debt to God. There was too much I wanted to know. Starting with the biggest question of all: why we are here in the first place?

Relax your body.

All is calm. All is bright.

Who are you kidding?

Don't go to sleep.

For in that sleep what dreams may come?

My eyes closed on me.

I woke up shivering. No way of knowing how long I'd been out. My stuck leg was numb. The warmth of the rocks was wearing off. I thought about the movie where the guy cut off his own arm to get out from under a big rock. What a great idea that would be. I could hop across the desert in the dark.

Of course, I had no knife. So that was out.

With the strength I had left I pushed and pulled. My leg didn't budge.

Starving to death. Now there was something to look forward to.

What of Ira? He'd be worried. He'd probably come out and ask around Dillard. Eventually, it'd get back to the sheriff and he'd be told *Mike Romeo? Never ran across him. Maybe he got into Las Vegas. Give us your card and if we hear anything we'll give you a call.*

But they wouldn't know that Ira can smell fabrications. He's like a hunting dog, always on the alert.

There was maybe a one in ten chance he'd find out what happened to me.

If he didn't, it would tear him apart.

I didn't want my only friend in the world to live with that.

. . .

My father, who for years taught a seminar on the *Summa Theologica*, was convinced that reason tenaciously applied got you to the place where you could no longer honestly deny the existence of a First Cause. And further, that an unbiased view of the evidence of design in nature—from the irreducible complexity of the cell on up—made the First Cause an Intelligent Designer.

From there, he always said the characteristics and name of this Being could only be based on faith. Upon what text or prophet or messiah would you place your faith?

My mother, who taught at the Yale Divinity School, embraced both mystery and liturgy. We had some good talks at night when I was young. I remember once when I was nine and she was tucking me in and I asked her if God created some people just so he could send them to hell. She asked me where I'd come up with that, and I told her I'd been reading one of her textbooks—I was that kind of nine-year-old—and that God decides who goes to heaven and who goes to hell, and we have nothing to do with it. And there was a preacher in America once named Jonathan Edwards who talked about sinners in the hands of an angry God. And he also said that if a father went to heaven and his unbelieving son went to hell, the father in heaven would be happy about it. It would add to his bliss.

Mom didn't hesitate. "Whatever God is like, he is certainly not like that. You can go back to the error of Augustine to trace that error."

That's how my parents and I talked to each other.

I did trace that error a few years later. I wanted to keep looking for the real character of God.

But then my parents were murdered and I stopped looking.

. . .

L ight woke me up. Light from the east. The sun was coming up on the desert. It should have been one of those beautiful sights you go *Aww* at. My stomach clenched like a fist ready to punch the rest of my guts out.

One more try on the leg.

No go.

There wasn't a cloud in the sky. Soon the sun would begin its full fry mode. I'd be an egg in the Mojave frying pan.

Scanning the horizon I couldn't make out a single sign of humanity, civilization, Native American history, Boy Scouts, military, even a bird.

I'd never felt so alone.

It was time to pray. What did I have to lose now?

And then, suddenly, I wasn't alone. I was joined by a furry friend.

T he desert tarantula is more ugly than deadly. At least, that's what I've read. Whatever natural selection or intelligent being concocted the design of these arachnids, it was done with the intent of making them as repulsive as possible. This one was a deep, rich brown, and seemed intent on inspecting me, for whatever instinctual reason coursed through its tiny brain. I'd had the same reaction from certain college professors back at Yale, but that hardly seemed relevant now.

This hairy spider was a big one. Fattened on large insects. Its four pairs of legs worked the rock like a pianist's fingers playing a Bach sonata. And while it might not kill me if it bit, there might be enough unpleasantness in the venom that I'd wish I was dead. It was coming at me from an angle just behind my right shoulder. I determined to make no sudden moves until I could give this creeping hairball a solid whap with the back of my hand.

If I'd been the kid I once was, maybe I'd entertain the notion of treating this thing like a science project. I knew there were guys out there who handled these pug uglies like little pets.

I was in no mood to experiment with it.

But apparently it had no such qualms about me.

I lost sight of it. My head wouldn't swivel that far.

Then came the first touch of spider legs on my back.

Did these things like blood? I doubted it, but wasn't sure. If they did, there was certainly a sumptuous picnic waiting for it on the side of my head.

"Okay, Fuzzy, take it easy now," I said, noting that I was probably about to go mad. "Nothing to see here. Move along."

The delicate feet continued their upward trek to my neck.

"We can be friends, but we need to give each other our own space. You can have all these rocks, Fuzzy. My body is off limits. How does that sound?"

Fuzzy said nothing. He was now at the base of my skull and seemed to be pausing for breath. Or looking at a map. Which way to go?

To the right he'd find my blood. To the left, my sweat.

I didn't want to risk a bite by making a sudden move or muffing a swat.

A long minute went by. It seemed in that minute the sun, directly behind me, upped its game to full blast.

And Fuzzy seemed perfectly content to camp where he was. Like he was getting a tan. I wondered if he was holding one of those little mirror things under his chin.

Did tarantulas have chins?

Something moved across the sky. A speck. A plane? No,

a helicopter. Too far away for me to signal. But waving my arms was out of the question for the moment. Fuzzy was not to be disturbed.

Even so, the odds of being spotted by anybody, in the air or not, were about the same as a one-legged kicker making the Packers.

With nothing better to do, I watched the helicopter float across the blue. It looked military. Probably connected to that base Ira told me about.

Then my eye noticed a glint. Something reflecting sun. Something green.

Glass.

A piece of shattered glass.

As if someone had used a bottle for target practice.

Somebody had been out here, maybe recently.

But who? And would they be back?

What about the deputy sheriff? Wouldn't he be back with an off-road vehicle soon?

Fuzzy started to move again. Over my left shoulder and down my arm. He was probably the last company I'd ever have so I thought about letting him stick. Instead, I waited until he was at my elbow, then with my other hand I flicked him off.

Fuzzy went flying onto a neighboring rock.

I hoped he wouldn't get mad and come back for revenge.

He landed on his back and wiggled his legs for a bit. I was a little sad about that. Far be it from me to confuse the little creatures of the earth. I'd rather concentrate on confusing thugs and—

Out of nowhere, a reptile struck at the helpless Fuzzy.

It was a snake.

A rattler.

And Fuzzy stopped moving.

. . .

R attlesnakes have a long and colorful history in our Old West folklore. Cowboys and horses hated them. But the Indians found these vipers helpful and healing. Chinese laborers brought in to build the railroads had snake oil with them, a venerable ancient cure. Into this mix came a new band of hustlers called snake oil salesmen, who went from town to town, claiming their elixir would work wonders on all sorts of ailments. What was in those bottles varied, but the least likely ingredient was actual snake oil.

Today, snake oil salesmen run for Congress.

In the deep south they have snake handlers, who misinterpret the Bible and let snakes bite them. Down there they also say a rattlesnake belt can cure "the rheumatiz," and if you have tuberculosis all you have to do is cut off a rattlesnake's head, put it in a jug of rum, and finish off the jug. Maybe it didn't cure you, but you probably didn't care for two days.

I had another idea for the rattler coming toward me. But first I'd have to catch it and kill it. And here I remembered something else. If you have to kill a rattler with your hands, you don't do it by the head. The head of the snake is made to bend in all sorts of survivalist ways, and you're as likely to be bit as not.

Instead, you need to grab it by the rattle end and then whip it so you snap the hyoid bone that connects the snake's head to its body.

These little bits of knowledge I'd retained from some previous text seemed, right now, to be of far more benefit than all of Plato and Aristotle. Being close to death focuses your attention.

I knew that rattlesnakes take up a defensive posture against sudden movement. But I wondered if some subtle moves could coax him over. Then again, what if he snapped at me? Part of me thought, well, if I got bit it would lead to an agonizing death, but at least it would be shorter in duration than starving.

What lovely choices we have sometimes.

I tapped the rock with my right hand. Here, boy. Here, Fang.

Amazingly, it worked. Fang left Fuzzy and started slithering toward me. Its lateral undulation was right out of a nature documentary. The little forked tongue stuck out, sniffing the surroundings. Snakes smell with their tongues. What sort of fumes was I giving off?

Fang decided to investigate. He was about four feet long, a pretty good size. I was going to get one chance at this, and mentally calculated the whipping motion I'd make. I did it in slo-mo a couple of times.

Fang got closer.

What I hadn't calculated was what I'd do if he came straight at me and made his way up to my face. I'd probably have to take the chance and grab his neck and squeeze—something I've fantasized about doing to politicians from time to time.

When Fang was about a foot away from me its head went up a little, like there was a built-in periscope in that triangular fang holder. The forked tongue slithered out and waggled.

He knew I was there. Snakes don't have great eyesight, but they can see bulk.

And a rattler can strike any bulk hard and fast.

Don't make him angry. Don't worry him. Don't fluster him. Don't talk politics.

He paused for a moment, then put his head down and moved ahead, grazing my right arm, which was resting on the rock. I fought the urge to pull it away. My practice with Fuzzy at keeping still was paying off.

But then again, Fuzzy was dead.

So now it was man against snake. I'm not into killing animals for sport. But when it's him or me, I choose the dominion theory of life. Darwin over PETA.

I'd have one chance at this. If I missed, Fang would either be long gone or have his fangs firmly implanted in my flesh.

The tail with the rattle was coming within my grabbing zone. I eyed it like Fang had homed in on Fuzzy. Fair is fair. An eye for an eye.

And then it was time.

The moment.

You own it, you better never let it go.

I turned my palm up and scooped the tail just above the rattle.

And then, as good as a lion tamer with Barnum & Bailey, I whipped Fang out and away and snapped his scaly body with a firm recoil of my hand.

No middle school bully with a wet towel in a locker room could have done it any better. The serpent's neck cracked and I had hold of a dead snake.

Which was now a lifeline. All I had to do was fling him out over that piece of glass and draw it toward me.

Easier said than done. One wrong angle and the glass could go sliding out away from me.

My first attempt went wide of the mark. The snake landed about an inch to the right of the piece of glass. On my second throw I got the accuracy right but the landing was a little hard. The piece of glass shimmied out to the left of Fang's body and almost went sliding off the rock altogether.

This necessitated a new strategy. Before I could risk another direct hit I had to tweak the piece of glass back to where it rested before. There was only one way I could see of doing this and that was to recreate the undulation of my dead snake companion, and hope that one of the oscillations would tap the glass back to the best spot. So I tossed Fang over to the left side of the glass and started wiggling its tail, creating a slithering motion. It was like what I used to do as a kid with our garden hose.

Thinking of that hose made me realize how thirsty I was. That was the main enemy.

Careful now. I flipped Fang to the right. A perfect strike. The piece of glass skittered back almost to its original position.

I was giddy. I wished somebody had captured this for YouTube. When you're about to die, I can now report, little victories like this can seem like the Kirk Gibson home run in the 1988 World Series.

I had learned something with the slithering motion. Instead of trying to toss the body directly over the glass I thought I could undulate the snake in an up-and-down direction, making a wave. And with the right timing and moving a little to the right, set him at rest upon the glass.

What else did I have to do with my time?

First, a couple of practice ripples. Getting the feel of the range and motion.

Snake-wrangler Romeo.

Now...

The first time was a near hit. Fang landed on top of the glass but just a little to the side of it. When I tried to pull the glass toward me it twisted in a counter-clockwise manner and then slipped out from under the snake.

But it was closer!

Only problem was it had gone a few inches to the right, and there weren't that many inches to spare until it would be too far behind me, too hard for my arm and my snake to make a realistic play for it.

Sucking some air into my dry mouth, I closed my eyes and envisioned the next move. The way I used to do it right before I went in the cage. Seeing the legs of my opponent and how I would take them out from under him. Visualizing the exact quadrant of his face where my fist would find purchase. Putting myself in the zone.

There was no greater need than right now to find a new zone. The snake zone. The reptile domicile.

With one more deep breath, I opened my eyes and let the serpent flop.

Perfect. Fang bisected the piece of glass.

No sudden moves now. I gently pulled and the glass gently responded.

Five seconds later I had a piece of glass in my left hand and a dead snake in my right.

This I called progress.

Now all I had to do was reflect sunlight in a direction where someone with the capacity and willingness to find me would see it.

Yeah, that was all.

The only real chance, I figured, was wherever that helicopter had come from. Right now there was nothing in the sky except a few cumulus clouds.

But having nothing better to do with my time, I began the refracting of the sun. I held the piece of glass, which was about three inches in diameter, between my thumb and middle finger. I calculated the geometry and the angle which would create the small dot of light that could be seen at a distance. Just how far of a distance I had no way of knowing. It could be that only a jack rabbit a hundred yards away would see me. But the phrase *beggars can't be choosers* seemed apt at the moment.

And so, for maybe half an hour, I put out my pitiful distress signal.

As the sun rose higher and hotter.

And began to bake my head into a soufflé.

I found myself unable to fight some final thoughts about death. How it comes to everyone and you can't fear it. You have the choice to die well or not. Ancients used to long to die in battle, fighting courageously. It's hard to summon up that feeling when you're stuck in some rocks and your carrion flesh will be a vulture magnet, and your bleached bones someday become objects of curiosity for amateur archaeologists—*Who was this rock man? How did he get here? What must he have been thinking.*

I'll tell you what he was thinking. This is the worst possible death. No glory. Slow and agonizing.

Tongue dry and thick.

Coherence getting fried out of your brain.

A tarantula who had lost interest and then its life.

A dead rattlesnake your only companion.

A useless piece of glass.

A chicken talking to you, saying, "What're you doin' there?"

Wait, what?

A talking chicken?

I blinked my eyes. They felt like empty cement bags. But yes, there it was, a chicken. Looking at me. Advancing slowly in that chicken-walk way.

Now I knew I was dead. So this is what you see as you die. Not a tunnel with a white light at the end. Not flowers or oceans or Jesus.

You see a talking chicken.

But ... wait ... there was someone behind the chicken.
A man.

He wore black boots, black jeans, no shirt, black skin, bald head, full gray beard. Something around his waist. A gun belt?

He started fading into a blur.

The blur came closer. So did the chicken.

The blur said, "Can you talk?"

I tried to say yes, but my tongue had abandoned the communication thing. No sound came out and my brain decided to turn off the lights.

The research on death experiences is, by definition, anecdotal. After all, how can you test and verify what is entirely subjective? There are no selfies in that undiscovered country. But maybe Hamlet was wrong to say, for sure, that it's a place from which no traveler returns. All I know is that when I regained consciousness it was with the belief that I had somehow made that round trip.

But where was my port of re-entry?

It was some sort of shelter. Chiseled in rock.

I was on my back. Pain shot from my left leg upward, and from the side of my head downward.

Dim light seeped in through a square opening in the chamber. The opening was supported by wooden braces, what you might see in an abandoned mine shaft.

I blinked a couple of times to clear my vision. Even the blinking hurt.

A wooden plank set on a couple of rocks made a crude shelf. It held a bunch of cans, some of which were stacked pyramid-style. Next to this impromptu pantry was a garbage bag. It looked full, though it was impossible to tell with what. Some camping gear—a Coleman stove, utensil

set, canteen—was set next to the food shelf. A rolled-up
sleeping bag lay near the braced doorway. Next to it was a
white plastic box with a red cross on it.

I heard a chicken cluck.

Chicken ... chicken ...

I saw it just outside the grotto. I'm not an expert on
analyzing the facial expressions of fowl, but the one, as far
as I could tell, was looking at me like I was some sort of
intruder.

It clucked again. A voice from outside the dwelling said,
"What is it, Bill?"

A second later a man came in.

And yes, he was shirtless and wearing a leather belt and
holster with a pearl-handled pistol in it.

"Let's get you some water," he said. His voice was deep
and smooth. He picked up a canteen and poured
water into an honest-to-goodness tin cup.

I tried to roll to the side and get myself up on one
elbow. Didn't make it.

"Hold on there, son," the man said. He came to me and
got down on one knee. He put his hand under me, just
below the head, and brought me up slowly.

"Have a sip," he said, and put the cup to my lips.

I took some in. It tasted chalky. My tongue was
surprised.

"Made it myself," the man said.

"Made?" My voice sounded like I was whispering
through steel wool.

"Distillery. Solar. Have some more."

He put the cup in my hands and I drained it. Chalky,
yes, but so good.

"Where am I?" I said.

"Can you sit up by yourself?"

"I think so."

He took his hand away, then sat on the ground cross-legged. He adjusted his holster accordingly.

"You know how close you were to doing the Dutch?"

"I believe I do."

"Lucky for you I saw the sun glimmer you made with that piece of glass," he said. "Yep, you are one lucky fella, Mike."

My astonishment was momentary.

"I looked in your wallet," he said. "You don't carry much around, do you?"

I shook my head.

"I like that," he said. "The simple life, right? Like Tony Bennett said."

"Tony Bennett?"

"Don't believe frettin' and grievin', why mess around with strife? I never was cut out to step and strut out. Give me the simple life."

"Who are you?"

"Ever hear of the Desert Fathers?"

I blinked a couple of times. "Christian ascetics. Third century."

"Man, that's right! You've got some education. I figured that, what with the Latin on your arm. Truth is over everything, something like that. I bet we could have a conversation. A real one. Bill and I don't talk much."

Bill the chicken clucked.

"You're an ascetic?" I said.

"Hermit if you like," he said.

"What do I call you?" I said.

"Noah," he said.

"May I have more water, please?" I said.

He poured more of his home brew H2O into the cup. I

drank it up. I handed him the cup and touched my head. It was wrapped in gauze.

"Did the best I could," Noah said.

My left leg was also wrapped up. And stiff. But I could wiggle my toes. "How'd you get me out?"

"Some pushing and pulling. I wasn't sure you were gonna make it. Didn't know if that diamondback bit you before you killed it. How'd you manage that?"

I made a whip motion.

He nodded. "That's the way, all right. Anyway, you're lucky I used to be a D lineman. You're a big guy yourself."

The chicken strutted over to Noah. He stroked it as he would a cat. "This is Bill."

"Friend or food?"

"Family," Noah said. "The only kind I got anymore."

"I was in a plane that went down yesterday," I said.

"Is that what all that was?" he said. "I saw some choppers out there. Was it a crash?"

"Emergency landing," I said. "I was on the plane next to a woman who needed some help. I tried to find out what happened to her. Nobody was anxious to help. Next thing I know a guy is trying to take off my head with a chain, and a sheriff and his boy want to get rid of me."

"Sheriff Cullen?"

"Yeah."

"Wouldn't put it past him," Noah said. "He threw me in the tank once, called me the ol' N word a couple of times for good measure."

"It was his deputy who shot me."

"Sam?"

"Sam."

"Was it just you and him?"

I nodded.

"I couldn't see who it was," Noah said. "Only taillights."

"You saw it happen?"

"I just saw the lights out there in the distance. Thought it might be some lost idiot. So I hopped on Crazy Horse. That's my Indian off-roader. I went to take a look. Maybe he saw my headlight and that spooked him."

"I heard you," I said. "That's why I stumbled for the rocks."

"Oh, man. I had no way of knowing."

"But you're the reason he didn't finish me," I said.

"Happy to help."

"Does he know you live out here?" I said.

"Folks do."

"He'll be back."

"Likely," Noah said.

I tried to get up. No use.

"You need a doctor, son," Noah said. "I don't suppose you want to go into Dillard."

"That wouldn't be wise."

"I could put you on the back of the bike, I guess, try to make it to Vegas. But you're in no condition. You'd fall off halfway there."

"You have any ideas?" I said.

"Yes indeed," he said. "Let's get some pinto beans into you and talk this out."

He opened a can of beans and poured them into a camper's cooking pot and placed it on the Coleman stove.

I said, "Mind me asking why you chose this life?"

"Not at all," Noah said. "Hate."

"Hate?"

"It's what I came out here to get away from," he said.

"There's plenty of it out there," I said.

Looking at the beans as he stirred, Noah said, "You want to stand up and fight. You do it for yourself or somebody else. But when the torches and pitchforks keep coming at you, it can wear you down."

"You got on the wrong side of a mob, huh?"

"Oh yeah. I was a school teacher. Fourth grade. Made the mistake of hugging a girl who was crying. Somebody saw it, reported it, next thing I know I'm suspended without pay. A woman started a campaign to get me fired. I'm a single man, she played that up big time. Danger to the kids. She won. They canned me."

"You surely had grounds for a lawsuit."

He snorted. "Was going to cost me a hundred grand to get a private lawyer to take the case."

"How about your union?"

"As worthless as flip flops on a duck. They'd only pony up ten thousand. And they weren't exactly excited about defending me. When nobody listens, it gets to be a nightmare, man. I had to get out."

"And you chose the way of the hermit?"

"It seemed kind of natural," he said. "My daddy used to take me camping in the desert."

"Still alive?"

Noah shook his head. "Both parents gone."

"Me, too."

He looked at me then, a kindred spirit. He took the pot of beans off the Coleman and poured them onto two tin plates. He put a spoon on one plate and gave it to me. Noah sat cross-legged on the ground with the other plate. Bill the chicken seemed momentarily content.

Those pinto beans turned out to be the world's finest meal. Sitting on the dirt floor with my back against the rolled-up sleeping bag, a plate of warm beans on my lap, I began to feel human again.

Noah said, "When I look out at the morning, that's the best time. Sunrise out here takes the breath out of my lungs. Especially when there's clouds out there, too, and everything is like fire—red and orange and blue, and most of the desert is still shadow. The light of the sun, before it gets to be the laser beam of death. You know what I'm saying?"

"I think I do," I said. "I see similar wonders where I live, at the beach."

"You one of those rich guys?"

"Far from it," I said. "It's a mobile home in Paradise Cove."

"Paradise Cove." He smiled and shook his head. "Of all the names of a place to live, that's got to be the best."

"It's a nice little pocket away from the snarl of Los Angeles."

"I want to go back to the beach sometime. But there's something so amazing out here. I mean ... have you ever been in love?"

I was about to say *sure* but stopped on the *S*. It would have been a throwaway word, not thought out, not giving my rescuer the dignity of a true response.

Had I ever been in love? When I was the pudgy Michael Chamberlain, my only real love was chess. I was scared of girls and knew they weren't pounding on my adolescent door in a mad scramble to get to know me. It was easier for me to work on the complexities of the King's Gambit than to try and figure out the impenetrable mysteries of girls. Later, when I'd become Mike Romeo and was fighting in the cage, the companionship of women was readily available, but transient and unthinking. It's a dark part of my life I now wish never existed.

So, had I ever been in love? I'd been on the shores of it, once, and that recently. With a woman named Sophie, back in LA, who I met at the Argo Bookstore. And as I thought of her face, the first time I'd laid eyes on her, the remembrance of a kiss, I knew that my flippant answer of *Sure* would not in any sense be truthful.

I said, "Yes."

"Then that's part of it," he said. "I'm in love with this place." He was about to take in another spoonful of beans when he paused. "I hear something."

I listened. Could not hear a thing.

"Oh yeah," Noah said, grabbing a pair of binoculars. Bill the chicken followed him outside.

Strengthened by water and beans, I managed to get to my feet. My leg was a tower of ache, but I could limp along. With my head bandaged, I imagined I looked like the piccolo player from the Spirit of '76.

I ducked out of the grotto and found Noah scanning the desert with the glasses.

"Yep," he said. "Off-road Jeep. Sheriff's."

"How many?" I said.

"I think just one. Heading this way." He lowered the binoculars. And drew his pistol. He held it pointed at the ground. "I should probably turn you in," he said.

His friendly, bearded Buddha face was gone. He looked sad more than anything else.

"Really?" I said.

"If I hide you or help you, I'm involved. And if I get involved, no more peace and quiet."

"Probably true," I said.

"I mean, I don't know if you've been straight with me or not."

"Why wouldn't I be?"

"You could be a serial killer."

"I suppose anything's possible."

"Or an ax murderer."

"I'd make a pretty good ax murderer, Noah. But I have not made that a career choice."

"You could kill me *and* Bill."

Bill clucked.

"Or," I said, "you could choose to believe me."

Noah looked out at the desert, then back at me. "If I did believe you, what would be your plan here?"

I said, "If it's the deputy who tried to kill me, I'd like to talk to him. You can tell him the guy he's looking for is here, and then bring him in."

"What good'll that do?"

"I'll point your gun at him, disarm him, and have my little talk."

"My gun?"

"Which you'll let me have."

"I don't like that plan."

"You have another one?" I said. "One that doesn't involve turning me in?"

He thought about it. "Who was it that said no man is an island? Keats?"

"John Donne," I said.

He nodded. "Go back inside. I'll handle it from here."

"What are you going to do?"

"Better go. He's almost here."

From inside Noah's modest dwelling, I heard the Jeep come to a stop. A door opened and closed. I heard Deputy Sam's voice say, "Hello, Noah."

"Sam," Noah said. "What brings you out here?"

"Looking for a guy. A guy we arrested but got away."

"You think he's out this way?"

"Might have been this direction. Seen anybody?"

"I've seen you," Noah said.

"Come on, Noah."

"Tell you the truth, I have seen a guy."

"Yeah? Where?"

"In here. But he's not who you're looking for."

"Why not?"

"Because this guy's been shot. He almost died. Don't do that, Sam."

"What are you doing?"

"Put your hands on top of your head."

"Are you nuts?"

"Do it, Sam, or you'll die out here in a terrible accident."

Pause.

"Now turn around," Noah said. "Don't try anything dumb."

"This is not good for you, Noah."

Pause.

"Okay now," Noah said. "Inside."

With his hands on top of his head, Sam ducked in, followed by Noah holding his revolver in one hand and Sam's own sidearm in the other.

Sam looked at me like a frightened ferret. The resemblance was uncanny.

"What are you going to do to me?" Deputy Sam said.

"What do you think we should do to him?" I said to Noah.

"He's outside his jurisdiction," Noah said. "So maybe we should administer some desert justice."

"What are you talking about?" the deputy said.

"Explain desert justice to me," I said.

Noah said, "Well, first of all, you must kill anything that's poisonous that may try to bite you. If it's a snake, you kill it and then take off the skin and use it to make a belt or a hat band. You cook the rest."

Deputy Sam said, "The sheriff knows I'm here."

"But he doesn't know what you're going to find," I said. "Here's what I think you'll find. You'll find that I was still alive. But I was weak, crawling around in the rocks. You took out your gun and were preparing to finish the job when this Good Samaritan here shot you with his pearl-handled Colt. Then the two of us can report to the FBI exactly what happened. Two eyewitnesses to a rogue deputy about to commit murder."

Gears turned inside the deputy's head. I could almost hear the creaking. Then he said, "You're both crazy."

"And crazy people do crazy things, don't we?" I said.

Noah said, "Sure enough."

"But you might be able to survive all this," I said. "Interested?"

His eyes widened for half a second, then he squinted at me.

"I think you are," I said. "But I need to hear it from you."

"I'm listening," Deputy Sam said, trying to sound like a hard case.

"I want to know why you were told to smoke me."

Deputy Sam looked at the ground. I put my finger under his chin and tilted his head back up. "It's not a difficult question," I said. "You don't strike me as the type who's smart enough or has the cashews to shoot somebody on his own. You were acting on orders. Tell me who and why."

"I'm not going to tell you anything."

"Deputy Sam, do you want to die out here?"

"You won't kill me."

"Why won't I kill you, Deputy Sam?"

"Because you'd have everybody from the state police to the military to the FBI hunting you down."

"Let's see," I said. "I'm supposed to be dead. The way I figure it, everything that happens from now on is gravy. It might even be fun having people hunting me down. But I might as well make it worth my while by getting rid of one sorry excuse for a lawman."

I gave him my cucumber-floating-in-a-glass-of-ice-water smile.

For a long moment Deputy Sam swam in it, then said, "If I tell you, will you let me live?"

I looked at Noah. "Should I let him live?"

"That'd be fair," Noah said.

"All right, deputy," I said. "You have my word. But make it good."

"You were asking too many questions," Deputy Sam said.

"That's not enough. It was because I was asking questions about a woman named Karen Morrison, wasn't it?"

"I don't know anything about that."

"You've never heard the name Karen Morrison?"

"No."

"What about this guy Deveroes? Gus Deveroes at the hospital."

The deputy's eyes jiggled a bit. Then he said, "I don't know anything about him."

"You paused there, Deputy Sam. You're hiding something. That deal we had about letting you live may be off the table."

"We could tie him up to an anthill, Indian style," Noah said.

"All right, look," Deputy Sam said, "I don't know all about it. Deveroes may not be all clean. I don't know what he's doing, something with Medicare maybe."

"Insurance fraud?" I said.

"I don't know!"

"Because you don't ask?"

"What of it? I do my job."

"Whacking people is part of your job?"

"I was out of line," Sam said.

"Out of line?" Noah said. "That's what you call it?"

Sam's eyes darted over to Noah. Noah raised his pistol and pointed it at Sam's face.

"Easy, Noah," I said.

Keeping his eyes fixed on Sam, Noah said, "In the desert, no one can see you bleed."

"Put that down," Sam said.

"I don't think I will," Noah said.

I said, "Don't go that way, Noah."

"I'm too far into this now," Noah said.

"Make him stop!" Sam said.

"Noah," I said.

Noah put the muzzle an inch away from Sam's forehead and pulled the trigger.

There's a painting by the French artist Pierre-Paul Prud'hon, completed in 1808, titled "Justice and Divine Vengeance." It depicts a dead man on the ground, blood seeping from his neck, as his killer absconds with the man's belongings. Unknown to the killer, two winged angels pursue him.

The first angel is Divine Vengeance, who holds a torch to light the way. The other is Justice, who holds scales in one hand and a sword in the other. Prud'hon had been inspired by a line from the Roman poet Horace: "Retribution rarely fails to pursue the evil man." The murderer is not going to get away with it. Somehow, some way, he'll get his just desserts. The message is clear, O sinner—you can run but you can't hide.

For a time this painting hung behind the judge's bench in the Palace of Justice in Paris. It's a night scene, the murderer's face hidden in darkness, but the light of the torch will not let him rest in his desired isolation. When the sword of vengeance falls, his face will change, his realization will be a punishment even before the final sentence is carried out.

That expression, I imagine, will be exactly like that on Deputy Sam's face when Noah pulled the trigger of his Colt and the chamber echoed with a terrible and effective *click*.

And a pitiful squeal issued from Deputy Sam's throat.

"Guess I forgot to reload," Noah said.

The deputy fainted. This is sometimes the reaction, I'm told, when a guilty suspect is in an interrogation room alone, waiting for the inevitable grilling.

"Nicely done" I said. "You knew there were no bullets."

Noah smiled.

"Didn't you?" I said.

Noah smiled more broadly.

I took the handcuffs off Deputy Sam's belt and shackled him. "Let's wake the poor guy up."

Noah filled a cup with his chalk water and splashed it in Deputy Sam's face. Sam came to with a sputter, his eyes wide and fearful.

I grabbed him by the shirt and propped him against the wall of rock. He shook his head like a wet Chihuahua.

"Focus, Sam," I said.

"Whu...?"

"Focus. You're all right now."

"What...no..." He looked at his handcuffed wrists. "Stop."

"I'm going to need you to do something for me," I said.

He shook his head again.

"I'm going to need a statement," I said.

"Statement?"

"A written, sworn statement."

He blinked a couple of times.

"Two of them, in fact," I said. "One will be a statement about Sheriff Cullen ordering you to kill me. The other will be a confession."

He sucked in a labored breath. "There's...no way."

"Remember our deal?" I said. "About letting you live?"

From somewhere in the bowels of his lawman self-image, Deputy Sam summoned a defiant look and said, "I'm not giving you any statement."

"Then we'll have to kill you," I said.

"Let me do it," Noah said.

"No," I said. "I want to. It's my right. I'm the one he shot."

"But I'm the one with the gun. I just have to reload. Then I can shoot him and we can make it look like I was saving your life."

"Good point," I said. "We can work any forensics to match up with you doing the shooting. Where do you suppose would be the best spot? The side of his head?"

"I don't think so," Noah said. "That would look too convenient. I think right through the heart would be best."

"I agree," I said. "Nicely thought out, sir."

Our prisoner couldn't take it anymore. "Shut up, both of you! You're not going to do this."

"I guess we've got no choice," I said.

"Let's do this thing," Noah said.

"Go ahead and load your Colt."

Noah whistled as he popped the cylinder and fed it the ammo. He was whistling "Saint Louis Blues." Nice, slow rhythm. After each twelve-bar line he put in another bullet.

I watched Deputy Sam's eyes. He blinked hard after each tick of the entered round. His head jerked a little when Noah locked the cylinder in place with one flick of the wrist.

"I'm a little gimpy," I said. "Why don't you take him out and get him positioned. Put him on his back and I'll hold him down and you can give it to him. Then we'll position the body."

"Good idea," Noah said, holstering his gun.

It didn't take much effort for well-muscled Noah to take the pudgy deputy and escort him out into the sun.

Deputy Sam tried to curse like a brave man, but the words floated out on a squeaky whimper.

"Where should we do it?" Noah said.

"Over by the Jeep," I said.

Noah dragged Sam to the front of the vehicle. Then he kicked the deputy in the back of the knees, and down he went. Grabbing the back of Sam's shirt, Noah got him flat on his back.

I came up from behind and put my right foot on Sam's shoulder. My left leg didn't give me much support, but I managed.

"Put one in the heart," I said. "Then one in the leg. If we do it the other way he'll suffer too much."

From out of Deputy Sam's throat came the grunt of fear that comes out involuntarily when he realizes he truly is about to die. I've heard that a couple of times and it always brings out a little pity in me. But I'm practiced in tossing that pity aside into the lower regions behind my ribs where it dissolves in the acids of my stomach.

"Wait, wait!" Sam said.

"What are we waiting for, Sam?" I said.

"You'll kill me anyway, won't you?"

"We don't know each other, Sam, but believe me I don't want to kill you. I don't want to waste a life, even though you'll have a lot of work to do to make up for the mess you've made of yours. You give me the statements, and you will be delivered. It's a chance, a second chance at life. You might become another Camus."

"A what?"

"Tell you later," I said. "Now is the time of choosing. What do you choose, Sam?"

Half an hour later, in pen on a yellow legal pad, the shaky hand of Deputy Sam had written out, and signed, two statements.

I, Samuel Magnus, working as Deputy Sheriff under the command of Sheriff Lester Cullen, do state the following:

That on or about the 5th of September, I was ordered by said sheriff to take a man named Mike Romeo out into the desert and execute him. I did take Mr. Romeo out of town, but released him at a gas station thirty miles away on Highway 93. I am now afraid to return to Dillard and risk being shot by Sheriff Cullen. After signing this statement, I will be leaving the state. I am entrusting this statement to the safekeeping of the witness to this statement.

I declare under penalty of perjury according to the laws of the State of Nevada that the foregoing is true and correct.

Duly signed and dated and witnessed by Noah Bagley. The second statement was slightly different.

I, Samuel Magnus, working as Deputy Sheriff under the command of Sheriff Lester Cullen, do state the following:

That on or about the 5th of September, I was ordered by said sheriff to take a man named Mike Romeo out into the desert and execute him. I did take Mr. Romeo to a remote location, where he attempted to flee. I fired several shots, one of which hit Mr. Romeo in the head. I then left him for dead. My conscience will not allow me to live with this any longer.

I declare under penalty of perjury according to the laws of the State of Nevada that the foregoing is true and correct.

I folded the papers neatly and placed them on Noah's makeshift shelf and put a rock on top of them.

"Do I get to go now?" Deputy Samuel Magnus said.

"Not until we get a few things straight," I said. "You may be tempted to radio the sheriff, so we won't be letting you drive anymore."

"But how'm I supposed—"

"Relax, Sam. You're alive and the odds are you'll stay that way. You may also be tempted to try to get hold of the sheriff and lead him back here before I can do anything with these statements of yours. But right after we dispose of you—"

"What do you mean, *dispose?*"

"Easy, Sam. I mean it in the sense of get rid of, not destroy. English is such a fluid language."

Noah smiled. "I like the English language. I like the word *mellifluous.*"

"That's a good word," I said.

"Come on," Sam said. "Finish this."

"As I was saying, my witness here and I will be leaving to meet with my attorney, so I can deliver the statements to him. Any attempt on your part to circumvent our little arrangement—"

"*Circumvent* is a great word, too," Noah said.

"—will result in your confession going to both the state and federal authorities. See, I have a feeling there's some across-state-lines shenanigans involved somewhere—"

"*Shenanigans!*" Noah said.

"—and I'm going to find out what they are."

Any will to resist seemed to hiss out of Deputy Sam then, like a deflated tire.

"We're all dead," Sam said. "There's a guy. A big guy. I don't know all about him. I just know he's out there. He's not in Dillard. He may be in Vegas. I don't even know his name. But he's bigger than both of you, and that's for certain."

"And he is involved how?" I said.

"It has something to do with the hospital," Sam said. "Big stuff."

"Fraud?"

"I don't know. All I know is, if I try to run he'll find me. He'll find you, too."

"Then it seems to me," I said, "your only shot is to go to the feds."

"With what?" he said.

"You can get an investigation going."

"That'll put a target on my back."

"They can protect you."

"Yeah, sure. Why don't you just shoot me now and get it over with?"

"That's not a very manly response," Noah said.

"Huh?"

"Manly," Noah said. "You know, as in being a man."

"What does that have to do with anything?" Sam said.

"If you don't know, I can't explain it," Noah said.

I sat on the floor, my stiff left leg pointing straight out. "Let's be rational about this. You say your life is over, and that may well be. Why not see what you can do with it?"

"What're you talking about?"

"Camus said the one truly serious philosophical problem is suicide. Should you go on with life or not? But why choose *not?* Instead, why don't you see how far you can go? Make your life an experiment in action."

"You're one of the weirdest people I've ever come across," Sam said.

"Then join me in this grand adventure," I said. "Let's see what we can do. The worst that can happen is we end up dead."

"Great."

"Or you could end up with something much more valuable."

"What's that?" he said.

"Manliness," Noah said.

I said, "Does Cullen expect you to check in by radio or phone?"

Sam shook his head. "He doesn't want anything specific over the air or by text or email. He's very careful about that."

"But if you don't come in."

"Yeah, at some point he'll call."

"That buys us a little time."

"Time for what?"

"We're taking a trip," I said.

I had Sam unlock his phone, noting he used his left thumb for that. Then I took it outside and called Ira.

"It's me," I said.

"Michael, where—"

"I've got a situation here."

"Oh dear."

"A deputy sheriff in Dillard tried to kill me."

"Michael ... what?"

"I'll fill you in later. Right now I've got the deputy."

"Got?"

"He's sort of a reluctant witness."

"Oh no."

"Don't worry," I said.

"That ship has sailed," Ira said.

"The point is, he is willing to turn state's evidence, has signed a sworn statement to that effect, and needs our protection."

"Oh, is that all?"

"How long until you can get to Vegas?"

"Long? I ... well, five and a half hours, once I leave."

"How long before you can leave?"

"Really?"

"Trust me."

"Hoo boy."

"And bring me some clothes," I said. "All I've got is what I'm wearing."

"How are you getting to Las Vegas?" Ira said.

"Sheriff's Jeep."

"You're stealing a sheriff's Jeep?"

"Of course not. The deputy will be driving. At gunpoint, true, but—"

"Michael!"

"It's the best I can do in the circumstances."

Ira said, "I'm sure it has a dash-mounted GPS tablet. They can track that."

"We have a window of time. We're about an hour from Vegas."

Pause. "What phone is this?"

"The deputy's."

"They can track that, too."

"It's not like I have a lot of choices."

Pause. "Remember that gas station we tanked up at last time we were there?"

"How could I forget the Pump N Snack?"

"Just off the Las Vegas Expressway."

"Right."

"Okay, get there, then drive about two miles south on Las Vegas Boulevard to the Viva Las Vegas Wedding Chapel."

"Really?"

"Listen! There's a Thai place attached to it. Pull in that lot. I'll have someone there to pick you up. Leave the phone in the Jeep and go with him. Got it?"

"Got it."

"Then get going."

"You sure you don't want me to go with you?" Noah said.

"Bill needs you here."

"It's nice to be needed," he said. "You need a clean shirt."

He ducked back into his cave and came out with a long-sleeve flannel shirt. "I don't wear 'em much myself anymore. Take it."

I took off my dirty Hawaiian and put on the flannel. "Feels good."

"And don't forget these." He handed me the sworn statements. I folded them and put them in my shirt pocket.

"Well," said Noah, "that's it. Come back and see me sometime. We'll have some beans."

"Count on it," I said.

. . .

Deputy Sam drove. I sat next to him holding his weapon on my lap. I told him to get back on the main highway and head for Vegas. He looked tired, defeated, futureless.

"It's not that bad," I said.

"Yeah, right," he said.

"Why don't you tell me how you got involved with Cullen?"

"It's my job."

"Was."

"I am so dead," he said.

"How vain it is to sit down to die when you have not stood up to live."

"Huh?"

"I'm paraphrasing Thoreau."

"Doing what to who?"

"Henry David Thoreau. He actually said 'sit down to write,' but I think death is more applicable here. You're not ready to die."

"I don't want to," Sam said. "But I don't know what I'm going to do."

The desert was moving toward a twilight calm. You forget about snakes and tarantulas then. Almost.

"Where are you from, originally?" I asked.

"Reno," he said.

"Grow up there?"

"Yeah."

"How'd you end up in Dillard?"

"I applied. They had an opening. I didn't want to be in Reno where I know people."

"And where people know you?"

"I guess," he said. "Why am I telling you this?"

"We're on a long drive," I said. "Might as well pass the

time. Who knows? Maybe we'll find a way for you to stand up and live."

He didn't answer. We kicked up dust and sand for another couple of miles, then hit the highway. We were on our way to Sin City.

"I'm going to ask you an important question," I said. "I want you to think about it before you answer. You ready?"

"Probably not," he said, with a slight waver in his voice.

"Which is why you need to ponder it. Here it is. How on earth did you get to the place where you were actually willing to kill an innocent man?"

His shoulders tensed forward.

"Well?" I said.

"I don't want to talk about it," he said.

"Why not?"

"You make me nervous."

"That's a good start," I said.

"What does that mean?"

"Anxiety is the engine of philosophy. If we didn't get nervous about what we're doing here, we wouldn't think about it, would we? All I'm asking you is to think about it."

He thought about it.

"Think out loud," I said.

"Look," Sam said, "it wasn't anything personal about you."

"That's a little hard to accept."

"I do what I'm told."

"Why?"

"That's what you do."

"Did you get that from the little lapdog's book of rules?"

"Lapdog?"

"That's what you are, isn't it?"

"I needed the job," he said.

"So this is about money."

"Everything's about money."

"What about love?"

He snorted. "That gets you nowhere."

"Honor?" I said.

"That just gets you killed."

"Let me see if I've got this right," I said. "You want to stay alive for money, and don't care about love or honor."

"So?"

"And when the day of your death does come, what'll you have?"

The radio crackled. Cullen's voice said, "Sam, come in."

The deputy looked at me. "What should I do?"

"Make something up."

"You wouldn't shoot me over this, right?"

"Not if you make it sound good."

Cullen's voice: "Sam, come on, pick up."

I pointed the Glock at the deputy.

He took up the handset. "I'm here, Les."

"Are you coming back?"

"Yeah."

"When?"

"Soon."

"Good." Pause. "Good, right?"

"Oh yeah."

"Good."

"Ten-four," Sam said.

"Cut it out," the sheriff said.

Sam put the handset back. "He doesn't like procedure."

"I'm shocked," I said.

We drove on. With a little prompting, Sam gave me some of his background. Alcoholic accountant father, school teacher mother. His parents divorced when he was ten and his father forced the sale of the house. With the proceeds he went off to drink himself into oblivion, which he did. After two years of community college Sam applied for a job as a detention trainee in the Sheriff's department of Humboldt County. "I moved criminals around from jail to courthouse," he said. A few years later he met Les Cullen, who offered him an "honest-to-goodness lawman position."

"Was that just luck?" I asked.

Sam shook his head. "He said he knew about me from a former prisoner, a biker named Wolf—that was his handle, anyway—who I ..."

"Did a favor for?"

He looked at me. "How did you know?"

"Not a big leap."

"Well that's it. I came down here four years ago."

"And became a good little lapdog for Sheriff Cullen."

"Stop calling me that!"

"You're free now," I said.

"Some freedom."

"Despite your trying to blow my head off," I said, "I've got your best interest at heart."

"Why?"

"No man is an island."

He slapped the steering wheel. "What does that even mean, man? You keep saying these things!"

"There are more things in heaven and earth, Horatio, than are dreamt of in your philosophy."

"Stop it!"

I let him alone after that. We drove on in silence.

. . .

About thirty minutes later there it was, rising from the desert floor.

What is the draw of this neon oasis the GIs used to call Lost Wages?

Perhaps because it saves on world travel, for you may visit the Eiffel Tower, the Pyramids of Egypt, and even New York City—albeit in miniature—for just a few bucks in gas money. Even better, you don't have to pay big green to see a celebrity in a show, for you can do a selfie with one of the many impersonators on the Strip for a five-dollar tip. There's always an Elvis around, but if you look you might find yourself a Sinatra (the older woman's preference), a Taylor Swift (for the Millennials), and on occasion a Sponge Bob for the kiddies. Just remember, that's not the real Sponge Bob!

Then there's the trance of transience, the allure of the impermanent, the intoxicating scent of forgetfulness. What happens in Vegas stays in Vegas, unless some inconvenient phone video of you grinding with a leather-clad street performer happens to go viral enough that your wife sees it on Facebook.

I directed Sam to the Pump N Snack. It was right where Ira and I had left it. Then south on Las Vegas Boulevard until we hit the Viva Las Vegas Wedding Chapel. How many tequila-soaked nuptials had taken place here? How many pledges of lifetime loyalty uttered before heading off to the craps tables at Caesar's Palace?

Romance—you could almost see it rising off the chapel's façade like aromatic hydrocarbons from a petroleum processing plant.

We pulled into the Thai place, where there was ample parking, and the headlights illuminated a small, thin guy leaning against a black sedan. He wore a burgundy suit that almost glistened in the light, a black shirt, a green tie. His slicked-back hair might have been brick red without all the mousse. With a pointed nose and V chin he resembled a well-dressed rodent.

He gave us a thumbs-up sign.

We parked and got out. I held the Glock behind my back.

"You must be Mike," the guy said.

"Must be," I said.

"And this is the witness?"

"Sam," I said.

"Call me Cus," the guy said. "Cus Handler, your guide to all things Las Vegas. If you'll step into my chariot, we'll be off."

"Where we going?" Sam said.

Cus Handler opened the back door of the sedan. "Not to the Venetian, I can tell you that."

"I don't like this," Sam said.

"Don't panic on me now," I said.

"I haven't stopped."

We got in. Cus Handler shut the door and came around and got behind the wheel. "Many a fond memory here at the Viva Las Vegas," he said, starting the car. "Marriage is so optimistic, am I right?"

"Where we headed?" I said.

"I suggested the place to Ira," Handler said as he pulled out of the lot. "It's out in a real community. We have those, you know. It's not all glitz and glamour and doubling down here in Vegas. We got schools and malls and parks and Arby's and Mickey Ds and people who don't bet on anything. It's a good life if that's what you're looking for."

"How do you know Ira?" I asked.

"About seven, eight years ago, he hired me to pick him up at the airport and be his driver for a couple of days. Day two I was waiting for him to come out of a meeting. It's hot, I have the windows down. And wouldn't you know it? A guy tries to jack my car! Puts a piece in my face. I get out, he gets in. And then he gets a pile driver in the temple. Ira is at the passenger window and just speared the guy with one of his crutches. Like a ninja. Like his braces are weapons, not just something he uses to get around. The guy is reeling and Ira gives him another wham, and puts out his lights. We get a cop and that's that. We've stayed in touch."

"You're going to like Ira," I said to Sam.

"I don't think so," Sam said.

"Everybody likes Ira," Cus Handler said. "Unless they're trying to do you wrong. My suggestion is, don't try to do anybody wrong, capiche?"

Sam didn't answer.

The Belt Buckle Motel had a horseshoe shape, two stories, with red doors and a powder-blue exterior. A swimming pool with a chain-link fence was in the center courtyard. Cus had secured two adjoining rooms, 20 and 22. He unlocked 20 and we went in.

Cus handed me the two keys. "You're on your own now," he said. "Ira will be arriving soon. Anything you need before I go?"

"There a good place to get something to eat around here?" I asked.

"What do you like?" Cus said.

"What do you like?" I asked Sam.

"I don't care," Sam said.

"Chinese?" I said.

"Whatever," Sam said.

"There's a good Chinese place about four blocks from

here, Crown Wok," said Cus. "Try their scallops and beef
with black pepper sauce."

"Is there anything about Las Vegas you don't know?" I
said.

"Only the things not worth knowing," Cus said. He gave
a little bow, then left, closing the door behind him.

Deputy Sam Magnus was looking like death on a hot
plate, so I set him up on one of the two beds and
gave him the TV remote. He turned it on and scrolled
around and found a channel playing *Gilligan's Island*. He
settled on that.

I went into the bathroom and put the Glock on top of
the toilet and gave myself a look in the mirror. It was not
exactly the cover of *GQ* staring back at me. Especially with
the gauze around my head. I unwrapped it, revealing a gash
caked with dried blood. Could have been a lot worse. A
millimeter more to the left and that bullet would have taken
half my head off.

Using plain soap and water and a washcloth, I cleaned it
up as best I could. It was painful, but I thought about the
Civil War and how good I had it in a modern-day motel
with clean water. Those boys had dirt and disease and tents
and cold. And no *Gilligan's Island*.

I folded a hand towel, wet it, and pressed it to the side
of my head.

Back in the room I sat at the Formica table with the
Glock and a *Las Vegas* magazine. I tried to read a profile of
Kenny "Babyface" Edmonds while canned laughter and
inane dialogue about "little buddy" issued from the TV. But
at least Sam was, for a moment, in repose.

I read some more. Sam started watching *Green Acres*. We

didn't speak. I wondered how many marriages were like this.

Finally, there was a knock at the door.

I put down the hand towel, took up the Glock, and went to the peephole.

Ira Rosen was smiling right at me. I opened the door.

"Now let's set things right," he said. He came in, using his forearm crutches.

Sam got off the bed, looking a little spooked by our visitor. Ira smiled and nodded. In his mid-fifties, with bushy gray hair spritzing from under his yarmulke, and full mustache under dancing blue eyes, Ira looks more like a favorite uncle than a former Israeli agent.

"This is my witness," I said. "Sam Magnus. Sam, this is Ira Rosen."

They shook hands.

"What happens now?" Sam said.

"We all relax," Ira said.

"Yeah, right," Sam said.

Ira said, "There's an old Talmudic saying. 'If you lift the load with me, I will be able to lift it. But if you will not, I won't.'"

"You two are full of sayings, aren't you?"

"If the shoe fits," I said.

Sam rubbed his eyes.

"Let's all sit," Ira said.

We sat. Ira and I in the two chairs at the table. Sam sat on the edge of a bed. Ira looked at the Glock on the table.

"His," I said. "This is what he did with it." I pointed to the right side of my head.

"How's the rest of you?" Ira said.

"Leg hurts, but I can walk and I can think."

To Sam, Ira said, "Are you hurt in any way?"

"Just my freakin' pride," Sam said.

"That's easily remedied," Ira said. "Now, please explain how we have all come to be here in our various conditions."

In ten minutes, I gave him a summary of my arrival in Dillard and all that transpired.

Ira took it all in, then said, "So, our guest will be treated as MIA by his superiors—"

"Superior," Sam said.

"Ah. But you are coming along with us willingly, correct?"

Sam gave me a glance. I nodded.

"Yes," Sam said.

"And have a signed statement to that effect?"

"Two, actually," I said. I took the statements out of the pocket of my shirt and gave them to Ira. He read them both as Sam and I sat and watched.

"You thought this up yourself?" Ira said.

I said, "I'd make a pretty good lawyer, yeah?"

"I'm afraid you'd fail the ethics exam."

Deputy Sam snorted at that.

Ira said, "Anything else of evidentiary value in your possession?"

"Only this," I said, spinning the Glock on the table. Ira slapped his hand on it. "I'll take that."

"I'm really getting nervous," Sam said.

Ira used his calm, rabbinic voice, which can get an angry ferret to recline on a sofa. "Mr. Magnus, I am your advocate in this matter. Tell me, have you friends or family that may want to check on you?"

"I have a sister in Elko, but I don't talk to her much."

"Anybody else?"

"An uncle here in Vegas. Runs a magic store on Fremont Street. But we haven't seen each other in years."

"What about in Dillard?" Ira said.

Sam said, "A few friends." Then he added, sadly it

seemed to me: "Not anybody who's going to give a rip."

"Who has oversight jurisdiction over your office, Sam?" Ira said.

"You kidding?" Sam said.

"Ah," Ira said. "Small-town sheriff and all that?"

"Les Cullen's been sheriff there for fifteen years," Sam said. "The people like the order he keeps."

"What about city or county council?"

"Lockstep," Sam said.

"What about state oversight?"

"They sent down a commission, eight, ten years ago," Sam said. "Before I got there. Nothing came of it."

Ira said, "For the FBI or the U.S. Marshals Service to get involved, or some other alphabet agency, we'd have to show the state itself had some complicity, or evidence of an across-state-lines enterprise. Or something foreign."

"Foreign?" Sam said.

"Some international criminal enterprise," Ira said.

"Ha," Sam said. "Not in Dillard. But ..."

"But what?" I said.

"There is something going on with the hospital."

"What sort of thing?"

"I overheard Cullen once with Gus Deveroes. Deveroes is the guy in charge at the hospital. And Cullen said something that sounded like 'the raisin.' I got the impression he was talking about a somebody, and a somebody very important. Deveroes starts yelling at Cullen, saying he better not try to pull that on him."

"Pull what?" I said.

"I don't know. I didn't get it. But Cullen said he might just go to 'the raisin' himself and Deveroes said he better not."

"Raisin?" I said.

Sam said, "I couldn't figure it out, like it was code of some kind."

"Why didn't you ask Cullen about it?" I said.

"It was a meeting I wasn't supposed to know about," Sam said. "If Cullen wants you to know something, he tells you. If he doesn't want you to, he doesn't, and you better not ask him."

"At least we know it's not a mafia case," I said.

"How's that?" Ira said.

"Made guys don't usually nickname themselves after dried fruit," I said.

Ira sighed. He does that a lot when I'm around. I can't imagine why.

"I can't do this ish," Sam said.

"Ish?" Ira said.

"Ah, something my dad told me to say instead of the S word."

I said, "You don't say the S word, but you'll shoot a man?"

"I know," Sam said. "It's effed up."

"I approve of his language choices," Ira said.

"I can't do this," Sam said.

"What choice do you have?" I said.

"I can go back," he said. "We can just forget the whole thing. I'll make up some cock-and-bull story."

"You wouldn't last ten minutes with Cullen." I stood. "Ira, do your Ira thing. Talk to him."

"Where are you going?" Ira said.

"I need to exercise my leg."

"Don't get lost," Ira said.

"I'll follow the North Star," I said.

. . .

The night air was balmy and felt good. I walked through a residential area, giving the illusion of being somewhere normal. An illusion shattered by the distant glow of the Vegas Borealis—the multi-colored light show emanating from the big hotels on the screen of the desert sky. The thrum-beat of dance music vibrated from somewhere within that chromatic canvas. Though we were well off the Strip, the Strip is never off of you in Vegas, and it wants everyone within a fifty-mile radius to know it. It wants to enrapture gawkers from Des Moines and college boys from Boulder, Koreans with cameras to click and Texans with money to burn. Come one, come all, to a magic place that's more dangerous than Disneyland, more exciting than your favorite dance club, and a promise that you can have just about anything you want for a price.

My leg was stiff but manageable. My head wasn't throbbing but it was tender and wanted to be left alone for a week.

I came to a strip mall. In the corner was that place Cus Handler had mentioned. Crown Wok. I went in. It had half a dozen tables, two of which were occupied—one couple each. One couple was youngish, African American. The other was white, in their forties. The music piping through the system was authentic Beyoncé.

A young Asian woman with black-rimmed glasses and no smile said, "Help you?"

"Take out, please," I said.

She handed me a tri-folded menu. I gave it a scan and ordered Kung Pao Beef, Shrimp with Hot Garlic Sauce, and Buddha's Feast, which the menu described as mixed vegetables. They all came with rice, and I added an order of Lo Mein. There was a cooler with soft drinks and beer near the counter. I told the woman to toss in three cans of Orange

Fantas. In case you didn't know it, the only acceptable soft-drink pairing with Chinese food is orange soda. I could be a killer food critic.

I sat on one of the two diner chairs by the door while my order was prepped. The black couple seemed to be enjoying both their food and each other. The white couple ate but didn't look at each other.

Unbidden, Sophie jumped into my head. I looked at one of the empty tables and tried to envision me sitting there with her. What would we be doing? Talking? Laughing? Or would there be that suspicion she held about me, and thus an invisible wall between us?

Why would I even think she'd be with me at all?

Why was love such a mystery to philosophers and poets?

My mind clicked through some famous love stories—Tristan and Isolde, Antony and Cleopatra, Bogart and Bacall, then it took a turn down Keats Lane and Lord Byron Street, where I wandered around awhile looking at lampposts. Then Sartre showed up and threw a wet blanket on things, as he usually does. *You know, it's quite a job starting to love somebody. You have to have energy, generosity, blindness. There is even a moment, in the very beginning, when you have to jump across a precipice: if you think about it you don't do it.* That's from Sartre's novel, *Nausea,* which is what I was starting to feel when the woman told me my order was ready.

Four Styrofoam boxes and three paper boxes of rice in one big plastic bag. The soda cans in another bag. I took my haul back into the Las Vegas night. The food smell was a pleasant elixir for the jumbled thoughts of amour.

The footsteps behind me were another matter.

There's a certain sound to feet when their owner means to do business with you. Combined with the darkest part of

the street and a large cinderblock wall on my left, instinct
spun me around.

He was dark and sleek and was coming at me with a
weapon.

I had the bag of food in my left hand and jerked it up
just in time.

The guy drove a knife into my dinner.

In my right hand were the cans of soda, which I
whipped into the side of the guy's head. Orange Fanta
makes a great makeshift blackjack if you're ever in the need.

The guy stumbled off the curb but made a quick recovery, staying upright.

I tried to can him again but he jumped back like a cat.

Whoever he was, he was in shape.

"You want money?" I said. It was less a question than a
way to buy some seconds. I needed to form a battle plan.
Normally in a situation like this—unarmed facing a guy
with a knife on a dark street—the best course of action
would be to drop the Chinese food and sodas and run away
as fast as I could.

My leg was not going to let that happen.

I hate knife fights. Especially when I don't have one. It
means my odds of getting sliced, somewhere, are high. Only
a little less likely is getting punctured. I had nothing to
wrap my hand with, just two bags of takeout.

"What did he tell you?" the guy said, his voice a soft
purr. In the small splash from a streetlight I saw he had
black slicked back hair and wore a black turtleneck. He
wasn't a street thug.

"You got the wrong guy," I said.

"Romeo," he said.

"Who?"

He smiled.

Then pounced.

Which I expected, having sized him up as a pro. I feinted with the cans and he ducked, going low with the sticker. I moved out of the way like a matador. My cape was the bag of food. He hit it hard and the bag exploded and Lo Mein and shrimp and beef went everywhere.

Including his face.

Which I kicked with my right foot. But because my left couldn't plant strong, the kick was weak and barely stunned him. I tried a backhand swipe with the cans but he put up his knife hand and sliced the bag. The cans hit the sidewalk. One of them exploded, spraying orange soda.

Now I had nothing.

He knew I had nothing.

And made a thrust.

And slipped on the food on the sidewalk.

It was just enough for me to jump on him, clamping my hand on his right wrist.

We both went down. I was on top.

But not for long.

The guy was good. Obviously trained in the arts and in fighting shape. His face in the dim lighting did not seem at all troubled. Cool and efficient, he reversed my takedown and had me on my back. I still held his knife arm. But the leverage was all wrong now. And with, practically, just one strong leg, I was almost completely at his mercy.

The smell of garlic sauce and orange soda was strong in my nose. You reach for what you can in a situation like this, it's instinct, and my right hand felt the sidewalk for ... what? ... a handful of noodles?

My attacker gave me a solid punch in the face.

It was my first lucky break. Because if he'd have hit me in my head wound, I would have gone out like grandma's last light bulb. As it was, the pain was manageable and gave me an extra shot of adrenaline.

My third break was finding something on the sidewalk. The least deadly weapon imaginable, but beggars can't be choosers. It was a paper-wrapped set of chopsticks.

I had one good reverse in me. I'd have to make it work or I was going to lose a lot of blood.

You can feint even when you're being held down. You letup a little on one side and wait to sense the slightest overconfidence from your opponent. Then you strike from the other side.

In a fight, that only works once. If it works at all.

The risk here was I had to let up a little with my knife-side arm. Which meant everything would have to happen within one second.

The stopwatch started when I let his knife hand come down.

In the first half a second I used every bit of strength I had to scream in his face and freeze him.

In the other half second I jammed the chopsticks into his eye.

M y hands on his throat finished him.

The smell of garlic sauce and blood befouled the air.

Then a dog barked. High-pitched and unrelenting.

A woman holding a leash with some sort of terrier at the end of it was staring at me from about ten feet away.

The light wasn't good enough to get a real bead on her, but I heard her exhalation of fear between the barks. She bent down and picked up the dog, turned her back, and ran away.

I limp-ran back to the motel.

· · ·

When I got there the door was open. Ira was sitting on a bed, arms folded.

"He took off," he said.

"What?"

"Just ran out that door."

"You didn't stop him?"

"You may have noticed that my lightning-quick days are over."

"Sorry," I said. "I'm a little on edge. I just had to kill a guy."

Ira closed his eyes.

"And," I said, "we better get out of here now."

"Michael, did you really have to?"

"You know me," I said.

"Do I?"

Ira used a scanning device to make sure there was no tracker attached to his van. We drove into the night, further away from the lights of Las Vegas.

"He was a professional," I said. "He waited for the right spot. I didn't pick him up until he attacked me. He used a knife."

"How do you know this wasn't a random act?"

"He wanted to know what Sam told us."

"That answers that," Ira said. "But how did he find you?"

I shot Ira a look. "You know."

"Cus?"

"Who else?"

Ira shook his head. "If it was, they made him talk."

"Maybe we need to talk to him ourselves," I said.

"We need to think this through," Ira said. "How did you dispatch this would-be assassin?"

"It wasn't pretty," I said.

"The body is where?"

"On the street."

"No one saw you?"

"A woman with a dog," I said. "But it was dark. And she ran away."

Ira said, "What else about the dead man?"

"Good shape, in his thirties. Features a bit Asian."

"Mixed race?" Ira said.

"Maybe," I said.

"Pacific Islander?"

"Could be."

Ira was silent, his eyes on the road, his head spinning wheels.

"What are you thinking?" I said.

"Give me a moment," Ira said.

A minute passed, and I said, "Anything?"

Ira said, "Recall when Sam told us about 'the raisin'?"

"Yeah."

"Could he have heard *Eurasian*?"

"I suppose it's possible."

"Because if that's true," Ira said, "we could be dealing with some very serious ish."

W e passed a Comfort Inn. Ira made a U-turn and we pulled in. Ira got us a room. I was ready. I was starting to crash.

But not before Ira explained some things. "There's a Eurasian organized crime enterprise. Out of the former Soviet Union and parts of central Europe. Financial crimes mostly, enforced the old-fashioned way. As you may have found out tonight. They operate in the U.S. to the tune of hundreds of millions. Taken from businesses, investors, even taxpayers."

"Do we know who runs it?" I said.

"They're not hierarchical, like the mafia was. You won't see those family trees. They have cells, independent, each with its own boss. They're like tribes with warlords. Occasionally they rub up against each other, but mostly keep a respectful distance. The roots go back to the Soviet prison system. They banded together for survival, and then for profit."

"In prison?"

"There was a caste system in Soviet prisons. The *nomenklatura* were the higher-up, elite criminals. The lower levels served them, got into procuring them goods through the system, bribing guards, and making a thirty percent margin. Nice work if you can get it."

"Especially in the jug."

"The *jug* is not what you would call those hell holes. So when the USSR went down in '91, these Eurasian criminals came out like disease-bearing rats, and the cheese was there for the taking. All these industries and resources being privatized. They pounced on it."

"Not openly, right?"

"The tried-and-true method—bribing corrupt officials. It got so bad that Boris Yeltsin, the first president of Russia, said organized crime was Russia's number one problem. Can you beat that? A former big-time communist complaining about crime. The world was turning upside down. Well, the gangs spread out. That included the U.S. The groundwork was already here. Do you remember the refuseniks?"

I shook my head.

"Before you were born. In the 1970s the Soviet Union was denying all sorts of ethnic groups, especially Jews, permission to emigrate. When the ban was finally lifted,

Europe and the U.S. allowed refuseniks in with barely a nod. Naturally, some of them were criminals. So they were here when the Eurasian gangs moved in and have been only too glad to help them."

"So what are you thinking?"

"One of their major areas of interest is health care fraud."

He paused so my cogs and wheels could turn.

"The hospital," I said.

"Exactly," Ira said. "They can bill for services not actually performed. They can upcode, that is, bill for more costly services than performed. Waive co-pays and deductibles then overbill the insurance carrier. Kickbacks for patient referrals. Then there's the opioid market. Bulk order hydrocodone and oxycodone and distribute that out to drug couriers."

"Sweet."

"Unfortunately, we cannot further question our witness. Any idea where he might have gone? Back to Dillard, maybe?"

"Maybe not," I said. "He was scared. He said he had an uncle who ran a magic shop on Fremont Street."

"Maybe you can pull him out of a hat," Ira said, "while I go to the FBI."

"Tag team," I said.

"Now," Ira said, "let's go see if we can find Cus."

As we headed for a neighborhood in North Las Vegas, Ira said, "Cus Handler is a small-time wheeler dealer who has proved useful and trustworthy in the past. He's one of these guys who manages to scrape a living wage out of a number of sometimes questionable practices. But he's always been honest with me."

"There's always a first time," I said. "Maybe he thought information about Sam Magnus could provide some remuneration if given to the right people. That meant calling the sheriff's office in Dillard."

"He wouldn't have known about the Eurasians," Ira said. "Unless by sheer coincidence."

"It would have been a gamble had he known."

"God gives us freedom to throw our dice and gamble with our lives. I want to know if Cus was gambling."

"Why would he talk to us if he got pressured by the Eurasians?" I said.

"We know how to apply pressure, too," Ira said, then quickly added, "Subtle pressure."

"Might they be watching his house?"

"Let's find out. We'll take a slow roll past his house and check the street."

"And if we see something?"

"You get out and ask them politely to leave."

"I love this plan," I said.

"Alternatively, I know the head of detectives at NLVPD. We can have a patrol take a look."

As Ira turned the corner onto Handler's street, he said, "On the other hand, patrol is already here."

Two patrol units in fact. Four uniformed officers were talking on the sidewalk in front of a house. A small group of neighbors looked on.

"I'm guessing that's Handler's place," I said.

Ira pulled over to the curb. "I'm guessing he just rolled craps."

"Sit tight," I said, opening the door.

"Where you going?" Ira said.

"To be neighborly," I said.

I walked the half block to the outside edge of the gathered neighbors. There was a young couple talking to an older man. Their talk was animated, which is always a signal of people anxious to share gossipy info.

I came up beside them and said, "What's all this?" I tried to look innocent. Raised eyebrows and all that.

The old gent shook his head. "Poor guy."

"Killed himself," the young man said.

"We don't know for sure," the woman said.

"The cop told me," said the young man in a superior voice.

The woman answered with an equal tone of supremacy. "They can't be certain yet. It's too soon."

"Too much CSI," the man said to me with a smirk.

The woman rolled her eyes.

"Did you know him?" I said to no one in particular.

"To say hello to," the old guy said. "He kept pretty much to himself. Got the feeling he was kind of slick, you know the type. They are all over this town. But he seemed friendly enough. The world is a pretty hard place."

A paramedic unit rolled up. Two medics got out. One of the uniformed officers started filling them in.

I walked back to Ira's van and got in.

"Is it?" he said.

"The rumor on the street is suicide," I said.

Ira shook his head. "I doubt it."

"And we're on the radar of death, aren't we?"

Ira, cool as the Mossad agent he once was, said, "You want to pull out? You're under no obligation."

A little less cool, but still frosty, I said, "Do unto them before they do unto you."

"Not exactly Talmudic," Ira said.

"But pithy," I said.

· · ·

That night I dreamed. I was on *Jeopardy* and one of the categories was "Meaning of Life." I kept getting it wrong. Alex Trebek looked at me with pity. Then the show was over and I refused to come out from behind my podium because I was wearing only underwear.

When I woke up there was desert sunlight burning through the window curtains. I looked over at the other bed. Empty. I sat up and rubbed my eyes then felt my head and leg. The pain was there, but bearable.

Ira came out of the bathroom, looking fresher than anyone had a right to be under the circumstances.

"There's a shaving kit for you on the sink," he said. "Clean up as best you can. My investigators cannot look slovenly."

"Investig*ator*," I said.

"All the more reason."

I showered and shaved and fashioned a hairstyle that mostly covered the gash. Then I looked at myself in the mirror and heard my brain saying, So this is how it's to be, huh? Getting shot and barely surviving and running into trouble the rest of your life. What are you doing, man? Why don't you take a cue from Noah, go find a place to live alone and read and raise chickens? Or is this what is meant for you, forever and ever, amen? Maybe Ira's God doesn't play dice but plays roulette, and you came up 22 Black, the only slot you get, and you've got to play it out, whatever it turns out to be. What'll it be, Romeo? Fade away or lean in? Run from trouble or make more of it for the bad guys? What is it with you and this feeling of needing to right wrongs? Why can't you—

"What're you doing in there?" Ira said.

"Just putting on my face," I said.

I think I heard Ira sigh.

. . .

W e drove into downtown Las Vegas. Ira dropped me off at a corner near the Golden Nugget Hotel and Casino. Said he'd meet me back there in two hours. He went off to talk to the Federal Bureau of Investigation.

I descended into Hades.

In Greek mythology, Aristaeus was a minor God who was known primarily for his cheese making. He was a trust-fund god who thought he was entitled to everything, including another man's wife. He took a fancy to Eurydice, who was happily married to Orpheus, and chased after her one day. Eurydice, trying to escape, stepped on a poisonous snake. She died and went to Hades.

Orpheus was devastated. Being a musician, he played such a mournful tune on his lyre that the gods took pity on him and gave him permission to go to Hades to retrieve his wife. He found her and was allowed to take her back to the world on one condition—he could not look behind him to see if she was still there. But Orpheus didn't trust the gods, and gave one quick glance.

Eurydice was taken away from him forever.

As a kid, I wondered what Hades looked like. What did Orpheus see down there?

And now I know. It must have been very much like Fremont Street in Las Vegas. Into which I descended in a last-ditch attempt to find Sam Magnus.

To do it, I had to weave my way under the lighted canopy they'd put over the street so they could call it an "experience." A couple of screaming twentysomethings whizzed past on zip lines, arms out, trying to forget the money they shelled out for the ride.

There were restaurants, bars, casinos, and street performers. That is, if you use *performer* in the most expansive way possible. While there was a fine juggler, there was also a pot-bellied forty-year-old in a body stocking, wearing gossamer wings on his back and just standing there swaying to the music being piped in. He had an orange bucket set in front of him, upon which was written *The Tooth Fairy*. For that he expected novelty tips from tourists posing for pictures with him—*Wait till Aunt Millie gets a load of this!*

It was Mencken who said no man ever went broke underestimating the intelligence of the masses. The Tooth Fairy was doing his best to prove the axiom.

The guy a few yards away from him didn't even have a bucket. What he had was a smirk on his face, a baseball cap worn backwards (always a bad sign) and a giant facsimile of a male member, attached on one end to the front of his pants, and which he controlled via two handles sticking out of the other end. He moved the appendage around in time with the music. The Bolshoi Ballet it was not.

A couple of college-aged girls, sipping lattes, giggled at the spectacle, which made the priapic puppeteer smile more broadly. I was about to abide by the wisdom of *sua cuique voluptas*—"to each his own"—when I spotted a ten-year-old girl nearby, staring at the phallic exposition. The performer looked at the girl, his creepy smile still plastered on his face. A woman rushed over and grabbed the girl's hand and turned her around.

The giggling girls moved on.

That's when I became a theater critic. I walked over and said, "Performance over."

His smile faded and he looked at my eyes. Then he gave me a two-word answer. The wrong two words.

I grabbed the offending appendage and ripped it off his pants and out of his hands. I tore it apart. Stuffing scattered everywhere, like a sorority pillow fight.

The exhibitionist started screaming a series of words

inappropriate for children, of which there were several within shouting distance. I took hold of him by the throat with my left hand, stopping the sound and forcing his mouth open. With my other hand I shoved a wad of stuffing into his mouth.

The widening of his eyes made my heart sing.

"Find another line of work," I said, and let him go.

His head pitched forward and he started spitting out the stuffing. His face was a satisfying shade of red.

I turned to walk away and ran into a very large security man. He was black, dressed in black, and said, "You're gonna have to come along with me."

"I don't think so," I said. The adrenaline pumps were working overtime inside me and I knew I was on the brink of doing something I'd regret.

The appendage artist started with the words again, and demanded I be arrested.

The security guard looked like he'd rather be in Philadelphia. "Let's talk this over in the office," he said to me.

"Forget it," I said. "Let it go."

The street performer got in my face. "You owe me money!"

I backhanded a fist into his nose. He yelped, grabbed his face, and blood trickled between his fingers.

"Now you're coming," the security guard said, pulling a Taser from his belt.

"No need for that," I said.

I n the small, messy security office, the guard, whose name was Harris, said, "You shouldn't have hit him."

"I was in fear for my safety," I said.

Harris smiled and shook his head. "That's not going to fly with the police."

"So you're referring this to the cops?"

"Any reason I shouldn't?"

"Yes," I said. "It would be the wrong thing to do."

"Why wrong? You hit the guy. You destroyed his property."

"Do you have any idea what his 'property' was?"

Harris nodded. "We know him."

"And you let him perform?"

"No law against it."

"There's a moral law, Mr. Harris."

"This is Vegas," Harris said.

"There's kids out there," I said.

"They got parents."

"This town advertises fun in the sun for the whole family, and you give them that?"

"I don't make those decisions," Harris said. "And now I've got to figure out what to do with you."

"Hire me," I said.

"What?"

"I'll clean up this town."

With a laugh, he said, "Who are you? I mean, what's your business?"

"I keep to myself," I said.

"You weren't keeping to yourself out there."

"I have five rules I live by," I said. "The fifth is protect the children."

Harris leaned back in his chair. There wasn't that much room to lean. "Look, I'll let it go. I'm gonna get an earful from that guy. I'll try to calm him down—"

"Why don't you Tase him instead?"

"But I'm gonna have to ask you to leave Fremont Street."

"I have no desire to be anywhere near this street again," I said. "But I have to see one person. It's business."

"I thought you kept to yourself."

"Except when I do business," I said.

He shook his head. "Easiest thing to do would be turn you over."

"Do not seek an easy life," I said. "Seek to be a stronger man."

"Man, you talk funny."

"Philosophy," I said. "It's a comedy goldmine."

Harris paused, rubbed his head. "Let's get it over with. Who do you have to see?"

"The magic store."

"I'll take you. But you stay right with me."

I followed Harris through a subterranean hallway and out on a side street. We reentered Fremont Street and he walked me to Cups 'n Balls. He told me to go in and he'd wait until I was finished. Then he would make sure I vacated the premises.

It was a normal-looking magic shop. I know because I was into magic as a kid and for awhile frequented a shop in New Haven. This shop had a glass counter filled with tricks and paraphernalia—linking rings, cups and balls, decks of cards, silks, thumb tips. On top of the counter was a magician's close-up mat. And standing at the mat, casually shuffling a deck of cards, was a bearded young man dressed like a waiter.

"Would you like to pick a card, sir?" he said, spreading the deck, face down, in front of me.

To be sociable I removed a card. The three of diamonds.

"Now, place the card anywhere in the deck." He held the squared deck out to me. I slipped the three somewhere in the middle.

He pulled the deck toward him, turned it so the cards were face up, and spread the deck across the mat.

"Now, if you'll find your card and slip it out."

I smiled. "That was very good."

"It's not over yet. Go ahead and find your card."

"It's not there. You palmed it. You executed a very nice Hermann pass, palmed the card, and now you're ready to slip it into the wallet in your pocket."

Frowning, the young magician said, "You're in the business."

"I used to fool around with it," I said. "A long time ago."

He put the three of diamonds, which was in his right hand, back with the other cards. "So are you here to buy?"

"I'm here to talk," I said. "I'm looking for the owner."

"You have some business matter?"

"Personal," I said.

"Mind giving me your name?"

"He doesn't know me. I know his nephew, Sam Magnus."

The young magician frowned. "He in some kind of trouble?"

"Is there a reason you'd ask that?"

"Mr. Magnus isn't here right now. I mean, his uncle."

"But he'll be back. I can wait."

"I don't know—"

"I'll level with you. Yes, Sam is in trouble. Very bad, I think. And he's scared. His uncle is the only lead I have to try and find him."

"Maybe you're the one he's scared of."

"Look at my trusting face, will you?" I said. "And there's a security guard right outside the doors, see?"

He looked. "I had to ask. You never know."

"Here," I said. "Let me show you a pass I learned as a kid."

So I spent the next half hour jawing with a fellow magician and messing with cards. Once you're in the brotherhood, you can talk shop with any other magician in the world. We had to stop a couple of times because some tourists came in to look things over.

Harris, my security guardian, came in after fifteen minutes and asked me how long this was going to take. I told him to pick a card. I said if I can guess which card you pick you can go on about your business and leave me alone. At that point I think he was ready to move on anyway, and he laughed and said, sure.

I forced the king of hearts on him and went through the usual patter about reading his mind and so on. He was visibly impressed when I got the card right. Then he left, but not without warning me again to get my butt off Fremont Street as soon as I was done.

Finally, the owner showed up. He was tall, around fifty, bald on top with a Fu Manchu mustache. He wore a white silk shirt, black vest, red bow tie.

The young magician told him I was here to see him about his nephew, Sam.

"And you are?" the owner said.

"Call me Phil," I said.

"Call me Quentin," he said. He shook my hand and motioned for me to follow him through a curtained doorway that led to a back room. Here there were various stage props and larger magic items, including the jigsaw woman illusion.

"I used to do the saw-the-woman-in-half trick," I said.

"Oh?"

"Then she quit on me. She now lives in Tulsa and Dallas."

He nodded. "An oldie but a goodie."

"Just to let you know I'm one of you."

"What's this about Sam?" he said.

"I had some dealing with him in Dillard."

"Lots of people do," he said. "In Dillard, that is."

"I think he's in trouble."

Quentin gave me a purposeful look. "And just who are you, to be asking?"

"It's kind of a long story," I said. "But I work for a lawyer, and Sam came with me here to Vegas, under our protection."

He folded his arms. "You're going to need to spell that out."

"How close are you to Sam?"

"I'm not going to answer any more questions until I know exactly what's happening and why you're here."

"You haven't heard from him?"

"Did you not hear me?"

"I get it," I said. "You don't know me from David Copperfield. So what if I told you he is mixed up in some business with a Eurasian gang?"

He looked at me a good long time. "I can't talk to you."

"You know about it then."

"I don't know anything. Get out."

"Which tells me you know a lot," I said.

"I don't know you, I don't know what you're peddling."

"You're scared."

"Out."

"Sam's missing," I said.

Quentin walked toward the curtain, looked out, turned and came back to me. "I told him not to get involved."

"Involved in what?"

"Are you a cop or a fed, anything like that?"

"No."

"You could lie about that."

"I could," I said. "But I don't lie. Here's my card." I showed him the tat on my left forearm.

"What is that, Latin?" he said.

"Truth conquers all things."

"That's supposed to convince me?"

"It's all I've got at the moment," I said. "And Sam is in real danger of being killed. I almost was."

He shook his head. "A few months ago Sam blew in here wanting me to go see Penn and Teller with him. Said he'd show me a night on the town. I live here. I don't need any night on the town, and I don't need to see Penn and Teller again for the tenth time. He gets me to come with him for drinks and to watch him shoot crap. I don't need to see anybody shoot crap for the rest of my life, right? But he's flashing hundreds at me, and that's not like him. So I go along, figuring to keep an eye on him. I didn't like what I was seeing."

Quentin took out a handkerchief from his coat pocket. He didn't produce a dove. He wiped his forehead.

"So we end up at the Four Queens. He insists on going to a table and loses five hundred dollars in ten minutes. I take him away and sit him down and start to get the story out of him. He tells me he's got something sweet going in Dillard, working for the sheriff out there, getting nice little bonuses. I figured it had something to do with meth, which means bikers, but no, he said it was legit. That's the word he used, legit, and it all ran through the hospital."

"He said that? The hospital?"

"Got me thinking. So after he's gone I go to a guy I know, and he lays it on me there's a rumor going around about Eurasian gangsters coming into the state. He tells me these guys aren't anything like the old mafia. He said they're a whole lot worse."

"Did you ever confront Sam with this?"

"Once."

"And?"

"He told me to ... to mind my own business." He wiped his forehead again. "And that's what you should do."

"He's in danger," I said.

"I *know* that! What do you expect me to do?"

"Any idea where he might go if he ran off into the Las Vegas night?"

"I might know a couple places," he said.

"I'm all ears."

He shook his head. "That's as far as I'm going to go with you."

"If I was on the other side I would have stuck a gun in your face," I said.

"If I hear from him, and he wants to talk to you, how can I get in touch?"

"I'll have to call you."

"That doesn't exactly up the trust level," he said.

"I'm as sure a bet as you're ever going to get around here," I said.

"No such thing," he said, and I couldn't argue the point.

I didn't mind leaving Fremont Street. I went back to where Ira dropped me off. Behind me was a parking garage. Across the street was a parking lot in front of an establishment called U-Bet Pawn & Jewelry. Park your car, pawn your ring, go put it all on red. The rhythm of life.

A woman in sunglasses and professional clothes—beige coat and slacks, white blouse—came around the corner and stood near the bus stop, back to me. Her brown hair came down below her shoulders. She was tall, maybe five-ten, wearing flat shoes.

But no purse or briefcase or satchel.

"FBI?" I said.

She looked both ways on the street, the way a well-brought-up child would before crossing. Then she turned and said, "Impressive."

"That's me," I said. "Credential?"

"Of course." She took a wallet-sized holder and flipped it open. Her name was Damita Ramos. The picture didn't do her justice.

I said, "Mr. Rosen dispatched you?"

"That's right," she said. "I'll take you to him."

"Why the cloak and dagger?"

Agent Damita Ramos smiled. It was a nice smile. "It's been reported that you sometimes overreact."

"Ira chose his words judiciously."

"You do have every reason to be cautious," she said. "More than you realize. Shall we go?"

"What if I say no?"

"Why would you do that?"

"Because I have every reason to be cautious."

She smiled again. It was still nice. "All right. Would you like to speak to Mr. Rosen? He's in our field office now, waiting for us. I can put a call through and have him talk to you."

"That's enough," I said. "Let's go."

"This way." She started walking and I followed. We went around the corner and down half a block where a black sedan with tinted windows was idling. It had a fed plate. Damita Ramos waved to the driver and the doors unlocked. She opened the back passenger door for me and I got in. She closed the door and got in the front passenger seat.

"This is Special Agent Josh Muller," she said.

Without turning around, the driver said, "Hi." He was a balding man, not too wide across the shoulders.

"Anything you can tell me on the way over?" I said.

"We'll do this with Mr. Rosen present," Agent Ramos said.

The FBI building was a three-story job that looked like a university library, or office space for dentists, travel agents, and accountants. We passed through a security gate and parked outside, like a grocery shopper.

Inside at reception was a lobby of potted plants and landscape paintings and humorless faces at the walk-through security detectors. A huge, black FBI/Justice Department seal dominated one wall, looming over us like the eyes of Dr. T. J. Eckleburg in *The Great Gatsby*. Agents Ramos and Mullen presented two forms of ID to the security guards. I was then passed through the electronics and given the wand treatment on the other side. The man with the wand was enthusiastic in his work. At one point, going up my inner thigh, he came perilously close to ringing the church bells.

"After this," I said, "I usually expect to be taken out to dinner."

He didn't respond. But Agent Ramos cracked a smile.

We took an elevator up to the third floor, a cubicle-filled space where people could have been cold-calling with insurance or stock offers.

Agent Ramos led me down the hall, pointing to one room and saying, "This is one of our ELSUR offices."

"Electronic surveillance," I said. "Am I going to wear a wire?"

"We don't call it that anymore," she said. "It's all digital."

"Am I going to wear a digital?"

"Come along, please."

She took me into an interview room with a table, four chairs, and Ira Rosen.

"As your lawyer," Ira said, "I advise full cooperation."

Agent Ramos indicated a chair for me.

"I'm a cooperative fellow," I said, taking a seat.

Ira cleared his throat with theatrical flair. "And just so there is no hesitation about your cooperative spirit, I want you to know that while you have been out exploring Las Vegas, I have been here hammering out an immunity agreement of mutual benefit. Anything you say in answer to these questions will in no way be used against you in any court proceeding."

"Hold on there, counselor," I said. "Am I going to be interrogated as a suspect for something that shall not be named?"

"We already know about your encounter with a would-be assassin," Agent Ramos said.

I looked at Ira. "Loose lips?"

Agent Ramos said, "No lips at all. The killing is a local matter for the Metro police and we picked it up. We're only interested in one aspect. The man you killed was named Johnny Tan. He is a known hit man. The fact that you came out of it with your life is kind of impressive."

I said, "How do you know if I had anything to do with this notorious fellow?"

"He's always like this," Ira said.

Agent Ramos said, "The police have already figured out that the man who killed Johnny Tan had purchased Chinese food from Crown Wok. It wasn't that difficult with the boxes and the receipt in the bag and the food spread all over the sidewalk with the body. The police have a description of the man who purchased the food, and it fits you remarkably well."

"There are a lot of people as handsome as I am," I said.

"But do any of them assault street performers?"

She picked up a remote and hit a button, and the

monitor screen came alive with a video taken by a handheld phone camera. It showed one Mike Romeo taking to task, in a physical manner, a man purporting to perform something or other with a large, anatomical puppet.

"The police have this," said Agent Ramos, "we have this, Instagram and Facebook have it, YouTube has it, and while your face is not completely identifiable, your physique is rather plain. And, of course, there is the Latin script on your left arm."

I shook my head. "A guy can't sneeze anymore without the world knowing about it."

"This may be to our advantage," Agent Ramos said.

"Our?" I said.

"Mr. Rosen and I and Agent Muller have had a very interesting discussion. Agent Muller is a forensic accountant. His specialty is medical insurance fraud."

I said, "You think the hospital in Dillard is routing a lot of it?"

"Absolutely," Agent Muller said.

"Why don't you go out there and close the joint down?"

Ira sighed and looked at the agents apologetically.

"We don't care about the, um, joint," said Agent Ramos.

"We care about who's running the joint," said Agent Muller.

"You mean Gus Devaroes?" I said.

Like synchronized swimmers, the agents shook their heads.

"Deveroes is a small fry," said Agent Ramos. "We want the head of the snake."

"He have a name?" I said.

"We don't know the name," Agent Ramos said. "We just know he's out there."

"Out where?"

"That's what we're trying to find out."

"Well, good luck to you," I said.

"We'd like your help," Agent Ramos said.

"How?"

"As a cooperating witness."

"So you do want me to wear a ... digital," I said.

"We'd like you to try to strike a deal with Sheriff Cullen," Agent Ramos said.

"A sting?" I said.

"Exactly," Ramos said. "You're alive, you have statements from deputy Magnus—"

"But not Magnus himself," I said. "He could be back with Cullen."

"Or he could be running scared," Ira said.

"I will remind you," I said, "that Cullen tried to have me killed."

"There is risk involved, of course," Agent Ramos said. "And if you're compromised we will disclaim any knowledge of your existence."

"Gee!" I said. "Where do I sign up?"

"Mr. Rosen and our counsel will prepare an agreement," Agent Ramos said.

"Don't worry, boychik," Ira said. "I've got your back."

"Fine," I said. "Has anybody got pizza?"

It is to the credit of our Federal Bureau of Investigation that a large pepperoni pizza was ordered for their new informant. And while Ira was in the counsel's office, and we awaited the arrival of the repast, Agents Ramos and Muller began briefing me.

"The challenge," Agent Ramos said, "is going to be finding the right circumstance for your conversation. What we need in order to get a warrant is some sort of admission from Cullen, even if it is just an indication that he is considering your offer."

"Which is?"

"Money for silence," she said.

"Excellent," I said. "I haven't used my blackmailing skills in quite awhile."

Muller said, "Are you taking this seriously enough?"

"It's my manner, sir," I said, quoting Peter O'Toole in *Lawrence of Arabia.*

"I don't know if this is a good idea at all," Muller said to Ramos.

Ramos's face reflected similar doubt. "Josh, give us a few minutes."

Muller stood, left the room, closed the door.

"Some more personal questions if you don't mind," Agent Ramos said.

"What if I do mind?" I said.

"We have to know who we're working with. It's all routine."

"Nothing personal is routine," I said. "It's what makes us human."

"Mr. Rosen told us you are something of a thinker," she said.

"Only something?"

"It's a rare quality these days."

I shrugged.

"The Latin on your arm," she said. "That's unusual."

"A drunken classics professor gave it to me in a bar."

"Really?"

"No. But it sounds better than that I went to a tattoo parlor."

"I don't like this any more than you do, Mr. Romeo."

I nodded. "Okay. Shoot."

"Romeo is not your real name," she said.

"Is that a question?"

"We know you were once Michael Chamberlain. That

your parents were victims in that mass shooting at Yale, what, twenty years ago?"

I didn't say anything.

"Then there's a period where there aren't any records of Chamberlain of any kind. You emerge some years later as a mixed martial arts fighter named Mike Romeo."

"Okay."

"We asked Mr. Rosen some questions about you, but he said it would be up to you to answer them."

"I don't have a criminal record, if that's what you're concerned with. You won't be embarrassed in court by that."

"How many men have you killed, Mr. Romeo?"

"No comment."

She said, "You took out a very dangerous hit man the other night. You've done that before."

I folded my arms.

"I just want to know who I'm dealing with," she said.

"I'm not a killer, if that helps. I don't like it. I killed that guy because he was going to kill me. It's happened before. Not many times."

"We've had some CWs in the past who've liked being on our side a bit too much. That can cause problems."

"If you're asking me to try to keep from killing anybody, I'll go right along with you."

"Please remember," she said, "that it's information we're after, not intimidation."

"I'll remember."

"When Mr. Rosen gets back with the agreement, we'll—"

"If I sign on, I'm officially on board with the Federal Bureau of Investigation."

"In a limited capacity."

"Which would mean any illegal search or seizure by me would be subject to the exclusionary rule."

"Impressive," Agent Ramos said. "Did you study law?"

"I read books," I said. "And chat with Mr. Rosen."

"You're absolutely correct about that."

"So what if I don't sign on?" I said.

"Why wouldn't you?"

"Because then I can do whatever I see fit to get the information, and can later decide to give it to you."

She gave me a long, studied look. "My official position is that we do not sanction or condone anything like that."

"Perfect."

"And what equipment will you use?"

"I'm sorry, but I can't tell you that. You see, I'm going rogue."

"As you know, we can't help you. And Mr. Romeo, I—"

"Mike," I said.

She smiled. "I don't want you to end up dead."

"We're all going to end up dead," I said. "The only question is how you live until it happens."

I didn't sign anything, which did not please Ira. As we drove away from the FBI building, he lectured me again on the value of cooperation with federal authorities.

"Like the ones in the Richard Jewell case?" I asked.

"Don't be a wiseacre," Ira said, and then quickly added, "Which is asking green not to be a color."

"So help me prepare," I said. "I'll need one of your small digital recorders and some Blu Tack."

"I've got both," Ira said.

"That's why I asked."

"Anything else?"

"A car."

"Don't have one."

"Next stop, Hertz," I said.

I chose a red Sonata. Modesty is one of my strong points.

Ira gave me a phone and a recorder, a silver job smaller than a playing card. It fit easily into my palm and would allow me certain magician's moves.

"Public places only with this guy," Ira said. "And if you don't get what you want the first time, pack it in and head back here. Keep in constant touch."

"Yes, Dad."

"And none of this personal revenge stuff."

"Me?"

"You. Especially you."

I patted his cheek.

I got to Dillard a little after five. The sun was low but blazing. I saw a woman on the sidewalk with an umbrella. She stopped at a corner and a tumbleweed—an actual tumbleweed, like out of an old Western—blew past her.

This appeared to be the most exciting thing happening at the moment.

But I knew where to go to find more. Because, again like in a good Western, when you need to get an answer you hit the saloon.

A smell of stale beer and surreptitious cigarettes slapped me as I entered Biff's. With my eyes adjusting to the dim lighting I heard, "It's you! By God and buy American, it's really you!"

There was no mistaking the voice. Moochie, the old

coot who had given me a ride into Dillard after the emergency landing, was sitting at the bar, waving me over.

I sat on the stool next to him.

"We thought you were gone," Moochie said. "Just run out on us without sayin' good-bye."

"I was called away on business," I said.

The bartender asked what I'd like to drink. I told him water. He frowned.

"What kind of business would that be?" Moochie said.

"Aluminum siding," I said.

"Pish!"

The bartender set a glass of water on the bar top.

Moochie said, "I get the feelin' you're not here to socialize."

"That may or may not be the case," I said. "There are certain parties I want to see. Maybe you can help me find out the best way to do it."

The stool on my left scraped out, and Candy Sumner, the baton twirler, joined us. She wasn't dressed in spangles this time. She wore a nice, white blouse over black jeans. Her makeup was heavy, though. And it was obvious why. She was trying hard to cover a dark crescent under her right eye.

Candy said, "You back for good?"

"Depends on your definition of good," I said.

She pursed her lips as if to say ooooh.

"I'd like to have a conversation with your sheriff," I said. "I'd rather it not be at his office."

"Sounds like criminal intent," Candy said.

"That's rude," Moochie said.

"And suspicious," I said. "But I'm a law-abiding citizen."

Candy snorted. "Draw me a Bud, Kevin," she said to the bartender. Then turned to me. "I know some things."

"Better not flap your yap," Moochie said.

"I think yap flapping is a fine idea," I said.

"Not if you got a boyfriend who—"

"Shut up!" Candy said.

Moochie shrugged.

"Till Felton give you that shiner?" I said.

"You shut up, too," Candy said.

Kevin the bartender put a beer in front of Candy. She picked it up and took a healthy swig.

I took a drink of water and looked at the bar top.

"You have something to say?" Candy said.

"Me?" I said. "No."

"Go on," she said. "Say it."

"I'm just sitting here," I said.

"He's just sitting here," Moochie said.

Candy shook her head. "You can all go to—"

"Come on, now," Moochie said.

Candy Sumner looked long at her beer. I thought for a moment she was going to cry. Then she took a deep breath and looked at the mirror behind the bar.

"So what?" she said. "So freaking what? How do you end up in a place like this? This whole town, this stinking bar? I was good! I was very good, but that doesn't mean anything anymore. Maybe it never did. Fooling myself."

"This doesn't have to be the end," I said.

She looked at me. "What do you know about it?"

"You are the master of your fate and the captain of your soul."

Her mouth dropped slightly open. I noticed Kevin the bartender giving me the side eye.

"It's from a poem," I said.

"What's it mean?" Candy said.

"It means you don't have to just sit here and take it."

She frowned, took another drink. She shook her head

slowly, then drained the beer. Without another word she stood and walked out of the bar.

"I don't know what you just did," Moochie said, "but it don't look good."

"What do you mean?"

"She might say something."

"To who," I said.

"To Felton," he said.

"You think?" I said.

Moochie shrugged. "He's not somebody a gal should say things to."

"Excuse me," I said, and went out the door after Candy.

She was halfway down the block when I got to her.

"What do you want?" she said.

"I don't want you to misunderstand," I said.

"What business is any of this to you?"

"We were just having a drink," I said. "People say things."

"You say things you don't mean?"

"I try not to," I said. "I just don't want you to misunderstand."

"Then what do you mean? What was all that in there?"

"I mean you don't have to let Till Felton beat you up."

"I don't like you," she said. "I don't like the way you talk, like you know everything."

"I don't know everything," I said. "I do know some things."

"What do you want here?"

"Did Felton ever say anything to you about me?"

She didn't answer, but looked like she could have.

"He tried to take me out with a chain," I said. "Do you know about that?"

She hesitated, then said, "He said you tried to fight him, then Cullen came and took you in."

"You ever see him with Cullen?" I said.

"At the auto-body shop," she said. "Till does the county cars."

"Anything more?"

"Saying hello on the street, maybe. It's not like they're tight. Least I don't think so."

"You don't have to stay with him," I said. "There's help. I can get you help in Vegas."

"That never works."

"You've been through it before?"

"Mind your own business, why don't you?"

"I want to help," I said.

"Why?"

"Does there have to be a reason?"

"Yeah there does. Nobody does anything 'less they want something out of it."

"Not always the case," I said.

"Yeah, sure. Just leave me alone."

"You want that?" I said.

"Yeah," she said.

"Okay," I said. I took out my wallet and gave her one of Ira's cards. "If you ever change your mind, call him. He's who I work for. We'll come get you."

She took the card and looked at it. Kept looking at it. Like she was staring through it and looking at the sidewalk. Then, in a whisper, she said, "Cullen likes to take his dinner at the Longbranch. Late. Around eight. That'd be one place to find him."

She turned and walked quickly away.

. . .

B ack in the bar, I told Moochie, "I need somebody around here I can trust. Know anybody?"

He frowned for a moment, then his eyebrows went up. "You mean me?"

"How did you ever figure that out?"

"Sharp as a tack." He smiled. "Now what can I help you with?"

"Not here," I said. "Where can we talk a bit more privately?"

"I know just the place. Where's your car?"

"In front."

"Hop in and I'll come around in my truck. You can follow me to my place."

M oochie's abode was a little house that would've been fashionable in 1954. It had clearly once been painted a confident shade of red. Now it was the color of dried blood. Cactus was the only apparent flora, arranged in some sort of forgotten garden.

Other than that it seemed a fairly lively place.

Inside Moochie's it was mainly old furniture, a Frederic Remington print on the wall in a frame that hadn't been dusted since the death of John Wayne, and several multi-colored plastic crates piled on top of each other.

Also on the wall, mounted over the Remington, was what looked like a 12-gauge shotgun.

Moochie insisted I have a beer with him, and I complied only because I needed compliance from Moochie. He motioned for me to sit in a chair with zombie springs— pretty much dead but still able to move.

As Moochie shuffled into the kitchen I gazed at the Remington print. It was one of his cowboy-on-bucking-bronco paintings, done in his unmistakable style. In this one, the cowboy has long since lost his hat, but holds a small whip in the air as the horse puts every effort into unseating him. It's man and beast alone in a clash of wills, and only one can win. But they need each other. Without the horse, there is no cowboy, no cattle drive, no West-ward-ho. Without the cowboy, the horse is left to remorseless nature. Together, they help make a civilization.

Moochie came back in and handed me a can of Tecate. He lifted his own and said, "Here's to a virgin sturgeon."

"A what?"

"Caviar comes from a virgin sturgeon," Moochie said, lowering himself onto the apple-green sofa. "A virgin stur-geon needs no urgin', that's why a sturgeon's a very fine fish."

He drank.

"You know, Mike," Moochie said, resting the can of beer on his stomach, "you got to go down swinging. I mean, we're all going down. I'm on the real downside. But I want to go down swinging. Somebody wrote a poem about that once, something about going down mad against the night."

"You're thinking of Dylan Thomas," I said.

"I am?"

"Do not go gentle into that good night, old age should burn and rave at close of day."

"That's the one! My dad said it once, when we were sitting around the dinner table. He read it, in fact. I didn't remember the exact words, but I remembered the way he read it. What do you think about that, Mike? About going down?"

"If it's a matter of going down swinging, then the ques-tion has to be what are you swinging at? I don't think it's enough to rage against the dying of the light. You've got to leave a mark that will let others find the light after you're gone."

"You know where the light is, Mike?"

"Still looking, which is the point. You don't give up looking. The moment you do, you're at the mercy of the universe, and you know what? The universe doesn't care about you for one little second."

"What about God?" Moochie said.

"Are you a religious man?" I said.

"I never kicked God out of the equation."

"He may very well be the equation."

"What if he's a she?" Moochie said with a grin.

I smiled. "There's a good reason God is depicted as a he in the ancient book."

"Oh yeah?"

"Because the ones who need to be reined in by rules and regs are young men. They need the force of a father who can come down on them when they start being anti-social. Which is what they'll be if left to themselves."

Moochie nodded.

"It's like the painting there," I said. "A cowboy has to use every bit of his strength to tame the horse. A boy needs a father to tame his own wild nature. That's what the Ten Commandments were for."

"You've really thought this through," Moochie said.

"My employer is a rabbi. He's the one who explained it to me. It makes too much sense not to be true."

Moochie took a thoughtful drink.

"Do you have a PC?" I said.

"Is that a computer?" Moochie said.

"A personal computer."

"What other kind would I have?"

"And the answer is?"

"No," he said.

"How do you keep up with the outside world?" I said.

"All I need to know I pick up at Biff's," he said.

With another sip of beer, I pondered what to ask him next.

He beat me to it. "You work for the guv'mint, don't you?"

"Not me," I said.

"Who, then?"

"I'm on my own."

"I don't believe it."

"I'm sort of on my own."

Moochie scowled. "How much is sort of?"

"It's good for you not to know."

"What's that say on your arm again?"

"Truth conquers all things."

"Then it's good to know the truth, ain't it?"

"You could have been a lawyer," I said.

"Don't insult me. But you're in my house, I think I got a right to know."

"I don't want you to get in too deep. There are some bad people out there who would like to do me harm. Which is why I should get out of here."

Moochie stood, went to the wall and pulled down the shotgun. "I'm prepared."

"I don't want you to have to use that."

"Listen, my daddy was with Patton in Sicily. I did one tour in Nam. Let somebody try to get at me."

"I'm going to try to meet up with Cullen."

"What for?"

"I have something I'm going to try. Candy said he takes his dinner at the Longbranch."

"I do believe so, sometimes."

"Tonight, maybe?"

"Maybe," Moochie said. "Just what is it you have in mind?"

"Something sneaky," I said.

"I like it already." He smiled.

"If it works out, I'll be on my way back to Las Vegas."

"And if it don't?"

"I may need a few more days. What would you think about having a house guest?"

"Depends on how young she is," Moochie said. Then he threw back his head and laughed.

The Longbranch Steakhouse would have been barely a cut above a Sizzler in Los Angeles, but here in Dillard was probably considered high end. By which I mean it used stainless steel flatware and cloth napkins. The napkins were black and set on red-and-white checkered tablecloths. A giant set of steer horns hung on one wall.

I spotted Cullen and Gus Deveroes at a table under the steer horns. They were chatting away. I calculated that if I could remove the horns, I would be able to impale them both at the same time. That cheered me up a bit.

In my pocket I had the digital recorder with a good-sized dot of Blu Tack adhesive on it. I took it out and palmed it. I've been palming things like coins and candy since I was a kid magician. It's as natural to me as putting on a shoe.

A hostess who looked like a high school senior asked if I would like to sit at a table or at the bar.

"I'm meeting someone," I said. "I think I see him."

"Oh sure!" she said.

Since the place was done up cowboy-style, I ambled over to the table.

Deveroes saw me first. Cullen had his back to me. But when he saw Deveroes's face, he spun around.

"Boys," I said, pulling a chair from an empty table and joining them.

They each had a plate in front of them. Deveroes was working on hot links and beans. Cullen was having brisket. They were about halfway done.

"What's good here?" I said.

"What's he doing here?" Deveroes said to Cullen.

"Let me ask," Cullen said. "What are you doing here?"

"I heard this place has good ribs," I said.

"To die for," Cullen said.

"Well, I already tried dying," I said. "It didn't take."

"You can always try it again."

As I was contemplating a clever rejoinder, a waitress with a round, sunny face appeared with first-shift enthusiasm.

"May I bring you a menu?" she said to me.

"He won't be staying," Cullen said.

"Yes," I said. "I'd like to see a menu."

The waitress stood there in frozen confusion, finally settling on, "Should I give you a few more minutes?"

"That'd be great," I said.

Obviously relieved, the waitress scooted away to another table.

"On second thought," I said, "maybe I'll go grab a burger somewhere else. I just wanted you to know, and I'm glad Mr. Deveroes is here, that the easy money stops. We know the setup."

"We?" Cullen said.

I smiled. Not my charming smile. My haughty snoot smile.

Deveroes looked at Cullen with the opposite of a poker face.

"Just wanted to give you a heads-up," I said, "because heads are going to roll."

With my left hand I reached for a shaker of Lawry's Seasoned Salt sitting in the middle of the table. Classic magician's misdirection. As I picked it up, I leaned forward, as if to pontificate about the stuff. At the same time I used my right hand to stick the digital recorder to the underside of the table.

"This signature blend," I said, holding the Lawry's aloft, "enlivens not just meat, but french fries, too. Just like ethics enlivens the soul."

Deveroes looked like I'd poured salt in his hair. "You are a crazy man."

"He's not crazy," Cullen said. He touched his napkin to his lips. "Are you, Mr. Romeo?"

"I think I am a little touched," I said.

"But reasonable," Cullen said.

"I do love reason."

The waitress came back with a menu. Also a look of concern on her face, as if she expected trouble. I smiled as I took the menu. The waitress scooted away again.

"As a reasonable man," Cullen said, "we should be able to discuss things, right?"

I looked at the menu. "Maybe I'll have a quesadilla."

"I don't like this," Deveroes said.

"Relax," Cullen said. "Why don't we discuss this at my office, tomorrow, say around noon?"

"Discuss what?" I said.

"Whatever it is you think is going on. I may be able to disabuse you of wrong-headed notions you may have."

"Your office," I said. "You won't mind if I bring along a witness."

Deveroes moved like he'd sat on a pin. "Witness to what?"

Cullen put up his hand. "I'm sure he means someone else to be in on the discussion. Isn't that right, Mr. Romeo?"

I nodded.

"Legal counsel?" Cullen said.

"I'll let you know," I said.

The waitress returned, holding her pad like a shield. "Would you like to order something?"

"Peace on earth," I said, and got up. "But I didn't see it on the menu."

The poor girl gaped at me. I turned and walked out.

M y car was parked in front of the restaurant. I jumped in and drove quickly around the block. I parked where I could watch the lot in back of the restaurant. Ten minutes later, Cullen and Deveroes came out and spoke. Then Cullen got in his cruiser, and Deveroes got in his Cadillac. They turned right out of the lot, then right on the main street, Silverado.

I waited another five minutes, then cruised up to the restaurant. I went back inside and was met by the same hostess, who looked at me askance. I'm used to that.

"Forgot something," I said.

"May I help you find it?"

"I think I left it at the table."

Unfortunately, there was another couple sitting there. The man was, shall we say, ample. The woman was slight. They were the opposite of Jack Spratt and his wife. I started for the table, with the hostess scurrying behind me with a concerned look on her face. As if I was going to disturb a customer. Which I was. But only marginally.

I put on my charming voice. "Excuse me, folks, I think I may have left my phone here. Did you happen to see it?"

The man was as jolly as his amplitude. "I know how that

is, fella. I forget mine all the time, and the missus sure likes reminding me of that fact."

The woman spoke quickly. "I didn't see any phone on the table."

The hostess said, "Maybe somebody brought it up front. I can check."

I said, "I wonder if it could be on the floor," and at the same time lifted the tablecloth a bit to hide my hand going under the table.

Where it felt nothing but smooth Formica.

Being a polite chap, I asked the woman if she would mind if I took a closer look at the floor. She frowned, but got out of her chair, as did her large husband.

I went down on one knee to scan the floor. Maybe the thing had fallen off. But there was nothing there. I looked under the table and saw only a dry wad of gum.

"Thank you," I said. "Please enjoy your meal."

"We will, young man," the husband said. "Good luck finding your phone. If you ask me, we'd all be better off with the old days and phone booths."

At that moment the same waitress who had handled the table before came over. She did not look glad to see me.

"Did you happen to pick up a small phone off the floor?" I said.

"No I did not," she said.

The hostess said, "Let's go look up front." It was in the form of a command.

So up front we went. At the hostess stand she called to the bartender, another woman, and asked if anybody had left a phone with her.

Negative.

"If it turns up," the hostess said, "is there somewhere we can reach you?"

"You could call me," I said, "but I don't have a phone."

What was obvious was that my attempt at misdirection, which I was thoroughly convinced satisfied all professional standards of the close-up magician, had failed.

Now Cullen had it and knew what I was about.

I went outside and got back in my car and called Ira.

"Change of plans," I said. "They got the recorder."

"How?"

"Had to be luck. I was perfect."

"Explain, please."

"I stuck the dang thing to the table. They couldn't have seen me do it."

Pause.

"Pull out," Ira said.

"I'm not ready," I said.

"It didn't work. That's all you can do. Come back to Vegas. I'll meet you—"

"I have some unfinished business."

Ira issued a disapproving moan. "Whenever you say that, somebody gets hurt."

"As long as it's not me, right?"

"There's a sheriff there who wants you dead. You're in a small, desert town."

"I'll be careful," I said.

"What does that mean?"

"It means I'll wear plenty of sunscreen."

"Michael!"

"So it didn't work out?" Moochie said. I was back at his house. We were sitting in chairs in front of his cold fireplace. He had a can of beer in his hand. I took a pass.

"You could say that," I said.

"What was it you were trying?"

"Moochie, it's best that you don't know too much."

He slammed his beer can onto a table made of an old tree stump. "You said somethin' about trust! That's a two-way street, pal."

"It's for your own good," I said.

"I ain't been told that since I was five years old and my old man took out the wooden spoon to paddle my butt. So don't you start in."

"Okay," I said. "No wooden spoon."

He waited.

"Cullen tried to have me killed."

After a long pause, Moochie said, "If somebody around here told me that, I wouldn't believe 'em. But you don't strike me as a fella who'd say that and not think it was true."

"See the side of my head?"

"I was wondering about that, but too polite to ask."

"That's where Sam the deputy shot me."

Frowning, Moochie said, "What are you about?"

"What if I told you Cullen is dirty, and involved in something really big and bad?"

"I'd believe you," Moochie said.

"I don't want to say too much more, because I don't want you in a position where you'd have to lie."

"I can lie with the best of 'em."

"No doubt," I said. "But let me fill you in later, when the dust settles."

"*If* it settles," Moochie said. "And I don't want it to settle over your grave."

"On that we agree," I said. "Can I stay here tonight?"

"You can have the sofa. I cleaned it off just the other day."

"I'll take it," I said.

"What's your next move?"

"You know the hermit who lives a few miles out in the desert?"

"You mean old Noah?"

"That's right."

"He's a friendly cuss," Moochie said. "Haven't seen him in quite a while."

"You know how to get there?"

"His place? Nah."

"It was in a rock formation," I said.

"That narrows it down," Moochie said.

"I got taken there once."

"Oh?"

"By deputy Sam. That's where he shot me."

Moochie put his beer down and leaned forward. "If you have an idea where to point me, we can give it a try."

"Let's do that," I said. "Tomorrow morning. Then I have a date with Sheriff Cullen. I'll want you to come with me."

"What can I do?"

"Just be around," I said. "You have become something of a comforting presence."

He smiled and raised his beer. "Ain't been called that in ... well, ever!"

I n the morning Moochie made a pot of coffee that could have melted steel. He cooked scrambled eggs in a cast-iron skillet and made toast by hovering bread, held by tongs, over the open flame of a burner on the stove.

It was a glorious breakfast.

He asked me if I wanted to shave and I told him no, I was going to grow a beard like his. That made him happy, and saved me ten minutes.

We took off to find Noah's grotto a little after nine. There was no traffic in the desert, and the semblance of a road for about a mile out of town, then a lot of dirt and sand. Moochie's dune buggy handled the terrain in fine fashion.

I guided him as best I could remember. When we were pointed in the direction I suggested, I used his binoculars to try to find the rock formation I'd been wedged in. There appeared to be two possibilities near each other. A fifty-fifty shot. I had Moochie head for the outcropping to the left.

When we got there, I had him drive slowly along the edge of the bleached rocks, looking for telltale signs of blood. Nothing. We made a wide circle around the rocks, coming to the other side, but couldn't make out anything resembling a hermit hideaway.

"You sure about the location?" Moochie said.

"Only as sure as whether we have some sort of soul inside us," I said. "Which means not certain."

"You could've just said *no*."

"It's my manner. Let's check the other place."

"I got nothin' else to do today." He revved up his buggy and we kicked up sand for ten minutes. Finally, we got to the other outcropping. It felt familiar.

"I think this is it," I said. "Try that way."

My instincts were sound. After a slow, five-minute cruise I saw the opening to Noah's cave. We stopped and got out.

I ducked inside. It was trashed. It looked like a hotel room in a B crime movie after the thugs had taken it apart. The dirt floor was covered with books, some ripped, and the few items from Noah's pantry were dumped around.

"He must've took off," Moochie said, coming in behind me.

"He didn't take off," I said.

"You think?"

"I think something is rotten in Dillard."

"But Noah kept to himself."

I wasn't going to tell him about Noah being a witness to two sworn statements. Not yet.

"There's something missing," I said.

"What's that?"

"Noah has an Indian motorcycle."

"Yeah, come to think of it."

"Not here."

Moochie tugged his beard. "So maybe he rode out and hasn't come back yet."

"Or maybe whoever was here took it."

"And Noah, too?"

"Possible. But why toss his crib and find, or not find, what he was looking for, and then go to the trouble of taking a motorcycle, too?"

"Sweet ride," Moochie said. "Classic Indians are valuable."

"It doesn't make sense unless whoever it was had the intent at the outset. He'd have to have a rig to carry it. Like a truck, but one with a ramp. This is all speculation."

"I get the feelin' that's something you do a lot."

"So join me. Does that profile fit anybody you can think of?"

Moochie thought a moment. When he looked at me, I knew he was going to say the same name I was thinking of.

"Felton," he said.

I didn't answer because I heard a pathetic cluck.

"What's that?" Moochie said.

I went outside and Bill the chicken clucked again, weakly, and jumped a couple of inches. In his better days he would have done a couple of feet easy.

Moochie came out. "A chicken?"

"Noah's rooster," I said. "We need to bring him with us."

"How's that?"

"He hasn't been fed. Noah wouldn't have left him like this. I think I saw a bag of feed in there."

Moochie went back in as Bill the chicken gave me the side-eye

"Found some," Moochie said, and came out with a bag of Purina Flock Raiser Crumbles. I took a handful of it and tossed some of it toward Bill. He bobbed his head a few times, looked at me and Moochie, then at the food. Then he took a tentative step forward, eyed me again, and finally pecked a pellet. This seemed to please him. He pecked up some more.

"Now what?" Moochie said.

"At some point I'll reach out and grab him," I said.

"That's no way to catch him! Sheesh."

"I'm open to suggestions."

"You stay right there," he said. "And don't make any sudden moves. Oh, and give me your shirt."

"My shirt?"

"I'm not goin' to use mine. You want to take this chicken, we use your shirt."

I gave him my shirt.

He took it and walked away from Bill and me. Bill watched him for a moment, then went back to his lunch. Moochie made a wide circle and came up slowly behind the chicken, holding my shirt out like a net.

"This is for your own good, Bill," I said, just as Moochie captured him with my clothing. Bill squawked and fluttered in his temporary prison. He was the perfect metaphor of modern man.

The sun was high and hot when we got back to Moochie's place. For all the trauma, Bill weathered the ride pretty well. I held him in the shirt but with his head out so he could look around. He wasn't in the mood for conversation, but at least he could see.

Moochie had some chicken wire in his garage and set up a makeshift pen in his backyard. I set Bill inside. Then I got more feed and spread it for him. He paused, feeling his inner Steve McQueen and looking for ways to escape. After a minute he began to eat.

Moochie put a bowl of water in the pen. "Now he should be happy as a Hollywood actor with a new divorce."

"You're not the romantic type, are you?" I said.

"Only when swimmin' with bow-legged women."

Bill clucked.

I actually enjoyed the drive into town. We took Moochie's pick-em-up truck. Moochie was chattering away but I was thinking about what a waste of a good location this corrupt little burg was. Small towns allow small minds to run around with an inflated sense of importance and power.

The Sheriff's Office was on the south side of town in a squat, nondescript, sand-colored building. Functional and uninspiring. It had a county seal on the outside and two deputies at a desk on the inside. One man, one woman. The man was in his twenties and built like a football player just out of college who didn't get drafted by the pros because he was too small. The woman was mid-thirties and serious, as if she were doing something really important like upholding the law. In truth, they were both just upholding the desk for a boss who could push them around.

"Hello, Rand," Moochie said to the male deputy.

The deputy looked up from a computer monitor and gave Moochie a curt nod. Then he looked at me and his eyes became black ice. No doubt I had been described to him by the sheriff.

"This here is Rand Kinsey," Moochie said to me. "Good ol' boy from good ol' Dillard High."

"Long time ago," Kinsey said. He kept his eyes on me. "What's your business here?"

I said, "Didn't your boss tell you he had an appointment with me?"

Kinsey and the woman looked at each other.

The woman, who wore a name badge that said *Dunlap*, decided she would be the one to take control.

"No appointments scheduled," she said.

"When will he be back?" I said.

"No telling," Ms. Dunlap said.

I shook my head. "You know where he is, and why."

The two drones did not bother with an answer.

"Mooch," I said, "why don't you go grab us some lunch at the DQ? Bring it on back. We'll wait here for the sheriff to return."

"I'm sorry," Ms. Dunlap said, "but we can't let you do that."

"At least you're sorry," I said. "Which makes me feel a whole lot better."

"I think you'd better leave now," Kinsey said.

"That you think at all is amazing," I said.

This brought the little football player out from behind the desk. He rested the palm of his right hand on his sidearm.

"You want to make something out of this?" Deputy Kinsey said.

Moochie said, "Now keep your shirt tucked, Rand."

"Deputy Kinsey to you." Kinsey pointed a stubby finger at Moochie.

"No respect," Moochie said.

"Your move, cowboy," Kinsey said to me.

"I'm urbane," I said.

Kinsey obviously didn't know what that meant. His eyebrows pointed down.

"Get out," Kinsey said.

"Tell your boss something the boxer Joe Louis once said about Billy Conn, before their heavyweight match."

Kinsey and Ms. Dunlap looked like they hadn't heard of either one of them. Public education.

I gave a little jab to the air. "He can run but he can't hide."

"What now?" Moochie said. The day was hot and clear, without any wind. A sniper from two miles away could ventilate me.

"Let's go back and check on Bill," I said. "Then get in your dune buggy."

"What for?"

"I want to see the crash site. I want to go back to square one."

"How many squares are there?"

"That, Horatio, is the question."

"Horatio? Who the ... never mind."

When we got to his house we checked on the chicken. He'd eaten all the feed I'd given him, and his water bowl was empty. Moochie went in the house to refill it.

I knelt at the chicken wire. "We'll find him, Bill. Just hang in there."

Bill did not cluck, but he did look like he understood.

I called Ira.

"Nothing to report," I said. "I'll probably be here until tomorrow."

"Agent Ramos is getting a little anxious about this."

"That's her job," I said. "She's a fed."

"What can you tell me?"

"I went to see the sheriff at his office. He made it a point not to be there. I'll make one more attempt at him."

"What good is that going to do?" Ira said.

"I won't know until it happens. And just how are you filling your time?"

"I'm doing your job," Ira said. "I have a meeting with our witness, Dr. Bukowski, in an hour."

"Tell him I said hello."

"I will not. You come in and tell him yourself."

"Soon, Ira. Soon."

Moochie and I took the dune buggy to the crash site. The plane sat like a belly-flopped pelican on the desert floor. There was a small crew of about half a dozen people in various positions around the plane. They all wore dark blue T-shirts and khaki pants.

When we got to within twenty yards of the plane, a man in a baseball hat and shades put his hand up to stop us. On the right side of his T-shirt were the initials NTSB in yellow, and on the left an insignia—a U.S. eagle encircled by *National Transportation Safety Board.*

Moochie cut the engine.

"Can't be here, guys," the man said. He was about six feet tall and lean, maybe fifty and in good shape.

"I was on that plane," I said.

He paused. "Did you provide a statement?"

"Talked to a lawyer in Dillard, in the barn where they were taking things down."

"Fine," the man said. "Now I'll have to ask you to leave."

"How you gonna get that thing outta here?" Moochie asked.

The man, unsmiling, looked at Moochie, and said absolutely nothing.

"Tow truck?" Moochie said. "What's the protocol?"

"Guys, you have to leave."

I was looking at the plane and wondering why something bothered me.

"Let me ask you a question," I said. "Have you analyzed the flight path?"

The man didn't answer, but he did look like I'd hit some sort of nerve.

"We were coming from Kansas City," I said. "Doesn't it seem strange that we're so far south of Las Vegas?"

He paused for a long moment. "Sir, would you mind waiting here just a moment?"

"I've got all day," I said.

The guy turned around and walked toward the plane.

"You got his attention," Moochie said.

"Looks that way."

"You got a skill."

"Skill?"

"At getting attention."

"I'd like to retire that skill," I said.

"Some people got it, some people ain't."

A few more minutes went by. Then the guy from NTSB came back, with another man, older, taller, gray-haired, and in a shirt with another alphabet, FAA. He smiled as he put out his hand. "Jerry Bergson."

I shook. "Mike Romeo."

Bergson nodded. "Would you mind having a word with me?"

"Sure."

"Over here?" He put his arm out.

I said, "Mr. Harrison is my personal advisor. Anything you have to say can be said to him."

Bergson shot Moochie a look. "Why are you making this difficult?"

"Things have been getting difficult for me ever since I got off that plane."

"In what way?"

"I don't trust people in authority," I said. "Call it a personal quirk."

"You do know I have the authority to take you into custody," Bergson said.

"I don't want to be unpleasant," I said. "As Aurelius said, if there be any kindness I can do to a fellow human being, let me do it now."

Bergson's forehead furrowed. "Who?"

"Marcus Aurelius," I said. "Roman emperor. Stoic philosopher."

"It's his manner," Moochie said to Bergson.

"If you think this is funny ..." Bergson said.

"I'm all in for serious," I said. "But there are things happening I can't tell you."

"Why is that?"

"If I told you, I'd have to ..."

"Kill me?" Bergson said.

"Get very upset," I said. "See, you could be corrupt."

Bergson's face spoke again, like it had been slapped.

"Not that you are," I said.

He pulled out a leatherette case and opened it, showing it to me.

"Official looking," I said.

"Fair enough?" Bergson said.

"Do you have a partner with you?"

"Yes."

"Can I talk to him, too?"

"Her," he said.

"I'll wait," I said.

Bergson nodded at the NTSB guy, who I'd forgotten was standing there. He went to the plane. A minute later he came back with a woman in her thirties, who could have been Bergson's daughter. She wore aviator shades and an FAA shirt. Her hair was brown, straight, shoulder length.

"This is Agent Miranda McKenney," Bergson said. "Show him your credential."

She did.

"Enough?" Bergson said.

"What's up?" McKenney said.

"He your senior?" I asked her.

"Who are you?" she said.

"We're trying to establish trust," Bergson said.

"Is he trustworthy?" I said.

"Of course," McKenney said. "Tell me what I'm doing here."

"Good enough for me," I said. "You are both here to help law enforcement, probably FBI. You have the same suspicions about this landing as I do."

"And what are those suspicions?" Bergson said.

"Criminal enterprise, here and in Las Vegas. This plane goes down in a strange direction. One of the pilots dies of an apparent heart attack."

"You know this how?" Agent Miranda McKenney said.

"Now you give me some information," I said. "What's the status of your investigation?"

Bergson said, "I'm sure you know I can't give you that."

"And here I was being kind to you," I said.

"What exactly is your interest in all this?" Bergson said. "Who do you work for?"

"This has nothing to do with my work," I said. "Does the name Karen Morrison mean anything to you?"

The two agents looked at each other.

"Who is that?" Bergson said.

"A woman I was sitting next to on the plane. I don't know what happened to her."

McKenney said, "Was she injured?"

"Just shaken up."

"They should have checked her at the emergency post in Dillard," Bergson said.

"And then she disappears?" I said.

"What's that mean?"

"It means there's too much that doesn't make sense about this whole thing."

"Mr. Romeo," Bergson said, "what exactly are you doing out here?"

"Same as you. Gathering information."

"For what purpose?"

"It's personal," I said.

"He means it," Moochie said.

Bergson said, "You two look like you could get in a lot of trouble. I mean, there's some risk here."

I said, "As in people trying to kill other people?"

The two agents didn't say anything.

I could have mentioned the name of Agent Damita Ramos then, but that would risk taking away my lone wolf status. Either of them might be called in as a witness at a future trial, and say that I was working with the FBI.

Which is also why I refused to take Bergson's card when he offered it to me.

I said, "You know those movies where a guy says, This conversation never happened."

Bergson nodded. "Is that what you're saying?"

"I'm not saying anything. Never happened, remember?"

I gave a head nod to Moochie and started for the dune buggy.

"Mr. Romeo," Bergson said.

I turned.

"I'd advise you not to press on with this."

"You're very kind," I said. "Aurelius would approve."

As we drove away Moochie said, "Next move?"

"Lay low until dusk," I said.

"Then?"

"We go have a talk with Felton."

"About Noah?"

I nodded.

"He's not going to be in a talkative mood," Moochie said.

"We have ways," I said.

"What does that mean?"

"I try the bluff first. If that doesn't work, I go to persuasion."

"Part of me doesn't like the sound of that. But part of me loves it."

"Which part is winning?"

"I always go with true love," Moochie said.

I waited until the sun was drifting down. The auto-body shop was on one of the back streets of Dillard that kissed open desert. It was an isolated unit, no neighboring buildings. It was made up of a fenced-in yard, an office, and two large bays. The bay closest to the office was open.

Moochie had told me Felton sat in his office the last hour of the work day. He had one guy working for him who he usually sent home around four.

So Moochie had me hunch down as he drove through the open gate. Felton wouldn't be able to see me from the glass door of the office. The plan was for Moochie to go in and talk, while I slipped out and went into the open bay, which had a door to the office.

I gave Moochie one minute inside, then made my play.

Moochie stood between Felton and his view of the outside. I went into the bay. It wasn't the neatest shop I'd ever seen. There was a black BMW in the middle of things, hood up, sitting just outside a double-post lift. The smell of oil, gas, and paint thinner would've been a brain fogger without air flowing through.

I leaned against the wall, and listened to the voices through the open door.

"It's a '57 Plymouth," Moochie said.

"And you want to restore it?" Felton said.

"That's what I said."

"You haven't got any '57 Plymouth."

"Why would I say I did?"

"Because you're crazy. Don't waste my time."

"You want to see how much I waste your time? Take a look inside."

"What?"

"Come on, step inside and see what I got."

A shuffling of feet, then Moochie stepped into the garage. He had a smile on his face.

Behind him was Till Felton. He did not have a smile on his face. And the moment he saw me, he went pie-eyed.

He made a quick move to go back in the office. I grabbed him by the shirt and pulled him in, slammed him up against the wall next to a workbench. I put my forearm on his neck.

"Close up shop," I told Moochie.

He nodded and went out to the street to close the gate.

"This shouldn't take long," I said to Felton. He tried to move but all I needed to do was press a little harder on his windpipe and he got docile again.

Moochie came back to the garage and worked the door down. We were now in a private setting. I gave Felton some more air space and said, "You're going to tell me some things."

He coughed a couple of times. The last one was a little too theatrical.

"Man up," I said.

He shook his head.

"Don't make this hard on yourself," I said. "All you have to do is the right thing. You ought to try it for a change. It'll do you good."

"Whatta ... you want?" Felton said.

I went with the straight-on bluff. "First of all, where's Noah Bagley? We know you tossed his crib. What did you do to him? And listen, if you start denying things I'm going to get upset."

Till Felton told me what I could do with my upsetness.

"Now I'm upset," I said. I threw a little Shakespeare at him. "But I have reason to cool my raging motions, my carnal stings, my unbitted lusts."

Lovely is the look of a punk's confused face.

"But," I said, "you keep going down this line and I might turn off my rational faculties for five minutes. Now, what did you do to Noah Bagley?"

Till Felton told me what I could do to myself.

It was not, however, a denial.

I nodded and took a step back. I raised my left hand, open palmed, like I was asking to be called on by the teacher. The moment his eyes went to my palm, I clocked him with my right fist. He went down like a sack of fender tools.

There was a chain with two grab hooks on the work-bench. I took it.

Moochie said, "What now?"

I'd almost forgotten he was there.

"I'm improvising," I said. I wrapped the chain tight

around the groaning Felton's ankles, and hooked it. Holding the chain, I dragged Felton to the lift and wrapped the other end of the chain around one of the lift arms. I punched the button and the arm went up, up, up, with Till Felton hanging there like a side of beef.

His eyes were lolling around and he sucked for air.

"He needs an oil change and lube," Moochie said.

The left side of Felton's face, where I'd hit him, was already starting to turn purple. I tapped him on the other cheek a couple of times. A sound sputtered out of his mouth. It sounded like a blender with its motor on the fritz.

"Focus, Till," I said.

He blinked and made more blender noise.

"We can stay here all night," I said. "I need a workout, and you'd make a great heavy bag."

Consciousness of his precarious situation slowly moved into his eyes.

"Where's Noah?" I said.

In a wheezy whisper, Till Felton said, "Don't know..."

"Where is he?"

Felton closed his eyes.

"Wake up," I said.

His eyes opened.

"Where is he?"

This time when he closed his eyes, it was like an admission.

"All right," I said. "You just rest a minute."

To Moochie I said, "Keep an eye on our boy."

"Hoop-dee-do," Moochie said.

I went into the shop office. It had a big desk covered with papers, a coffee mug, a rag or two, and a laptop. The laptop was open. I sat in the squeaky chair and looked at the computer.

The browser was Google Chrome. It had four tabs showing, one of which was Gmail. The screen I was looking at had an array of photos of scantily clad teenage girls. I clicked over to his Gmail and looked at the inbox. Various emails, various subjects, none of which seemed relevant. A few from the same sender had swear words in the subject. I opened one. It seemed to be from some buddy on car matters and troubles with a particular woman, with a copious use of the B word.

Nothing from Cullen, unless he was using a ghost name. I clicked on his Google apps and opened up his contacts. I searched for "Cullen." No hit.

I scrolled through the contacts to see if anything jumped out.

Something did. *Sally Hoskin.*

Why did that name sound familiar?

Because it was the lawyer who'd briefed me after the crash.

So why should she be on Till Felton's contact list? Sure, it was possible she did some legal work for him connected to the body shop. But was there some other connection?

I went back into his emails and searched for Sally Hoskin. It brought up one email in the trash, labeled *(no subject).* The entire message:

Re: conference, please be advised that notes taken are work product and must remain confidential.

I n the garage, Till Felton was starting to wriggle like a large carp. He cursed and screamed at us to get him down.

Moochie said, "He's recovering his personality."

I motioned for Moochie to come into the office. I handed him the laptop and told him to put it in his car.

"Stealing?" he said.

"Borrowing," I said.

"Oh, in that case." He took it out the front door.

I went into the garage and said to Felton, "One more chance. Where is Noah Bagley?"

"Let me down!"

"Sorry, that's not my specialty. I'll make sure someone checks on you, though. And one other thing, take away any thoughts of doing anything about this with your little friends or with your sheriff overlord."

Moochie said, "I don't think he understands that word."

"Do you understand me, Till?"

"Let...me down."

"Yeah, no." I motioned to Moochie for us to go. I killed the lights in the garage and the office. Till Felton was still yelling when we got outside. Moochie opened the gate then came back to the truck.

"You're not gonna leave him hanging, are you?" Moochie said.

"I'm tempted," I said.

"What if he gets down? Calls Cullen?"

"Good," I said. "That'll get me a meeting."

"Cullen could throw you in the clink."

"He won't. Felton's attacked me before. I got witnesses. Erotica writers from Oklahoma."

"The what with the who now?"

"Let's let him think about it for awhile," I said. "He may be more talkative if he thinks he'll be staying there all night."

.   .   .

A s Moochie drove us away I called Ira.

"Checking in," I said.

"What's going on?"

"I just interviewed a potential witness."

"To what?"

"I'm not sure yet. He wasn't cooperative."

"Uh-oh. What did you do?"

"He's all right. I'm going to take another shot at him in awhile."

"Shot?"

"Meanwhile, see what you can find out about a lawyer named Sally Hoskin. She was taking names after the emergency landing. She may be connected to all this."

"Hoskin?"

I spelled it.

"Michael, I want you out of there."

"Soon, Ira."

M oochie drove on till we reached a spot where the town was behind us and the desert in front. He cut the engine and said, "How long we going to give him?"

"Twenty-five minutes," I said.

"How'd you pick that number?"

"Random."

"Won't his head explode?"

"The human body is an amazing thing. The vascular system makes adjustments depending on circumstances. In this one, it slows the flow at the same time it puts out a distress signal. The upside-down body can last a long time if the heart is healthy."

"What were you in a past life?" Moochie said.

"You believe in that?" I said.

"It's possible, isn't it?"

"I guess you can't rule it out completely."

"I sometimes get a feeling I was in the Civil War."

"Did you survive?" I said.

"Don't know," Moochie said. "What about you? What do you think you'd a been, if it was real?"

"No idea."

"I think I know."

"Yeah?"

"A gunslinger," he said.

"Wild Mike Romeo?"

"Riding into town, taking on the crooked sheriff."

"What if I just delivered pizzas in Des Moines?"

Moochie shook his head. "Not you. No, boy, not you."

We talked a little more about the past. Moochie missed going to Dodger games back when tickets were affordable. What did I miss? Fishing with my father. Talking with my mother. And thinking there was a place in life where I might reasonably fit.

Then we drove back to the auto-body shop. Moochie parked as before, and we entered the office through the unlocked front door. The door to the inner garage was open. I felt for the switch and turned on the lights.

Till Felton was still hanging there.

Only now, directly under his head, was a big pool of blood.

Moochie was right behind me. "Holy mother of pearl," he whispered.

"Stay here," I said. I approached the body, being careful not to get near the blood. I circled around and saw an ugly wound in his middle. The blood had poured down and was covering his face.

"What do we do?" Moochie said.

"Get out of here," I said.

We did.

M oochie was subdued driving back to his place.
"I hate to say it," Moochie said, "but he got
what he deserved."

"But by who?" I said.

"That's the question."

"It happened fast," I said. "We weren't gone that long."

"Nope."

"I imagine he had some enemies in this town."

"More than a handful," Moochie said. "Now what?"

"I don't know. I need time to think."

"You can call your friend, the rabbi."

"I'll do that, as soon as I figure out how I'm going to put
it. He's not going to be—"

"Look!" Moochie hit the brake.

The flashing blue and red of emergency lights were a
hundred yards ahead, about where Moochie's house was.

"It can't be," Moochie said.

"It is," I said. "Turn around."

"We going to go on the run?"

"We're going to Las Vegas," I said.

"Check," Moochie said. "I'll have to get some gas,
though."

"Let's be quick about it."

Moochie made a three-point turn.

Bright, oncoming headlights blasted into my eyes.

Moochie cursed and stopped the truck.

The headlights remained on us.

Then the sound of a voice on loudspeaker: "This is the
county sheriff. Get out of your vehicle slowly, with your
hands high in the air."

Moochie looked at me. "What do we do?"

"What the man says," I said. "Unless you want to shoot it out."

"With what?"

"Exactly."

I opened my door and got out, hands up.

Loudspeaker: "Turn around. Get on your knees. Keep your hands in the air."

I did.

"Face down on the ground."

I kissed the earth.

A moment later I heard the vehicle door close, and the crunch of footsteps. "You're both covered," a voice said. "Do not move."

"That you, Rand?" Moochie said.

"Shut up!" the voice said.

"What's this about, Rand?" Moochie said.

"I said shut up!" he said.

"I want my lawyer," I said.

"You shut up, too."

"Very un-*Miranda* of you," I said.

"Shut it!"

"Not to mention the First Amendment."

He didn't respond, which made me feel great, all things considered.

About a minute went by, then another car approached. It had the light bar going. It stopped. Door opened, door closed.

More crunching footsteps.

Then the voice of Sheriff Les Cullen. "Well, look what the coyote dragged in."

"What's this about?" Moochie shouted.

"Put cuffs on both of 'em, Rand. If they resist, I'll fire."

"Moochie, don't say a word to anybody," I said.

That got me a kick in the side from Cullen. "You keep your mouth shut."

"You hear me, Moochie?" I said.

"I hear you," Moochie said.

Another kick from Cullen.

"You need more training," I said.

Kick. Fire under my ribs.

"We can do this all night," Cullen said.

Considering it was a long night ahead, I shut up. Rand cuffed my hands behind my back. He told me to get up. I did. I spit some dust out of my mouth.

Sheriff Cullen was a few yards away, caught in the ghostly cross-section of headlights.

"Put Harrison in yours," Cullen said.

"Remember, no talk," I said.

Cullen said, "What am I going to do about you?"

I didn't answer.

As soon as Moochie was secured, Deputy Rand came back.

"Put him in mine," Cullen said. For show he aimed his pistol at me, two-handed grip, like he was auditioning for a TV cop show.

The deputy guided me to the squad car and pushed me in the back seat and closed the door.

Following my own advice, I didn't say a word as Cullen drove off.

He wasn't chatty, either.

When we got to the sheriff's station, Cullen called for another deputy to come outside and meet us. It was the woman named Dunlap. With Cullen again holding his weapon out for all to see, he had her take me to an interview room.

She sat me down in a chair behind a metal desk. Then she left and closed the door.

There was a camera in one corner of the ceiling. Other than that, nothing else in the room except another chair and a table.

A few minutes later the door clicked open and Cullen came in. He closed the door and slid the other metal chair out from the table. He sat and put his elbows on the table and rubbed the bridge of his nose with his left hand, as if trying to stave off a headache.

"Romeo," he said. "You're a problem."

"Why am I cuffed?" I said.

"We'll get to that."

"That should be the first thing out of your mouth," I said. "Am I under arrest?"

"It sure looks that way."

"The charge?"

"It's very bad," Cullen said.

Drawing things out for his personal enjoyment. What a bore.

Cullen said, "You think you're a big, tough guy."

"Not true," I said.

"No?"

"I identify as a petite Asian woman," I said.

Cullen shook his head and gave me an annoyed half-smile. "And your mouth. You think you've got such a great mouth."

"My lips are a bit coquettish, sure."

"Why don't you tell me where you've been for the last several hours?"

"Aren't you forgetting something?"

"Your rights?"

"Just to make it official," I said.

He said, "It's just you and me, talking."

"It's me in handcuffs and you interrogating."

"You know what your rights are."

"I just like to hear law enforcement officials say the words. It's comforting. It'll also help your video."

"The camera isn't on. People trust me."

"I want a lawyer," I said.

"We all do, at one time or another."

He paused, stood. He walked around the table and came up behind me. I didn't swivel my head. I looked down and used my peripheral vision to watch his feet. But I lost sight of them just before a cannonball exploded into my kidney. I heard a guttural sound come out of my mouth, like I had a wounded bear in my throat. Pain shot through my spine and blasted a hole in my head.

It took me a while to get my breath back. Little fireflies flew around behind my eyes, dripping acid.

Cullen came back into view. Brass knuckles gleamed in his right hand.

"Old-school cop stuff, huh?" I said.

"Doesn't have to be," Cullen said.

I calculated my odds. I could probably get Cullen with a leg lock but what good would that do? There were deputies outside who'd hear any commotion. But then again, maybe Cullen's methods didn't sit well with them. Getting them into the room would at least give me a couple of witnesses.

I said, "Maybe you should give me a hint as to what you're talking about."

"You know," Cullen said. "You know very well."

"Why don't you fill me in?"

"Till Felton."

"What about him?" I said.

"You know."

"How do you know I know anything?"

"I just do," he said.

"You'd flunk freshman philosophy, Cullen."

Cullen huffed, shook his head. "Come on, now. Why'd you kill him?"

"Who?"

"That the way you want to play it?"

I said nothing.

"Or was it Moochie Harrison who did the deed?"

I didn't move or speak.

"Could have been Harrison, I guess," Cullen said. "After all, we did find Felton's laptop in his truck."

I'd forgotten about that.

"Looks bad for him," Cullen said.

"What do you want?" I said.

"Things are going to get unpleasant for you," Cullen said. "You can lessen the impact if you tell me why you're here, who you're working for. I might be able to get you to keep your life."

"Like last time?" I said.

"I don't know what you mean," Cullen said.

"You'd have failed acting class, too."

Cullen got to his feet. And began circling behind me again. I pushed myself back in the chair and saw he had a leather blackjack in his hand.

Talk about old school. Those things can put you under. For good.

Cullen had a smile on his face.

Not many choices here. I'd have to figure out a way, handless, to take him out completely, find cuff keys, unlock myself from behind, and make it through a couple of armed deputies.

Or I could scream bloody murder.

Which is what I did.

Cullen just stood there and let me.

A couple of seconds later Deputy Rand burst into the room, gun in hand.

I got in the first word, "He's crazy!"

"Shut the door, Rand," Cullen said.

The deputy started to step out of the room. Cullen said, "With you here."

"Oh," Rand said. He shut the door.

"The arrestee just made an attempt to escape," Cullen said.

I rolled my eyes. "I've got a bridge in Brooklyn I can sell you, Rand."

"He is not being compliant," Cullen said. "Kindly make him comply."

Rand looked confused for a moment, then it dawned on him. He holstered his weapon and removed a stun gun from his belt. He pressed a button. It snapped to life.

"I'll make you eat that," I said.

Rand looked at the sheriff.

"Go on," Cullen said.

"But how?"

"He doesn't have hands, Rand. Just do it."

The deputy looked back at me. I gave him the Mike Romeo stare. That froze him.

"Rand?" Cullen said.

Now he took a step at me. Mistake. He should have come at me like a bull. That was his only chance.

I kicked his hand. The stunner went flying into the wall. Cullen jumped back, as if my leg was firing volts.

Would that I could. My options weren't much at the moment.

Cullen shook his head like a disappointed father.

He pointed his gun at my head. "Get on your knees."

"Shoot me," I said.

There was a slight furrow of his eyebrows. "I said on your knees."

"I said shoot me."

"You think this is a bluff?" Cullen said. He took a step and had the muzzle a foot from my face.

"Whoever's pulling your strings doesn't want me dead," I said.

His face tightened.

"So I'm right," I said.

I enjoyed that moment. Too much. Because I didn't catch Rand coming up behind me and zapping me to my knees. I can take some voltage, but the surprise put me down.

Cullen clocked me good and hard with his gun.

And just before I blacked out I thought, *This is getting old.*

Your head can only take so much. The brain is a delicate melon, caressed by soft membranes encased in a sphere of bone. The whole setup is to protect your delicate brain matter. So it's best not to do things that slam it against the cranial wall. Like become a linebacker. Enough battery and down the line you can get Chronic Traumatic Encephalopathy, or CTE, which will drive you crazy. And the hell of it is, CTE can only be diagnosed after you're dead.

Which, when I came to, I wished I was. My head was a hot throb of eye-watering pain. My side felt like a horse kicked it. Every breath was a stab in the ribs. I was in a bed. When I tried to touch my head with my right hand, I couldn't. Because my right wrist was shackled to the metal side rail.

I was in a small room. No windows. Some shelving.

No idea how much time had passed.

The door opened.

My sight was clear enough to see it was a man in a suit. A dark blue suit. Dark blue tie with yellow stripes. Hair was black and perfectly coiffed. Sharp nose, eyes like laser beams. Smart, city boy.

"How we feeling?" the guy said.

I think I grunted.

"Been through a rough patch."

"Who ... are you?"

"A friend," he said.

"You don't look like a friend," I said.

"What do I look like?"

"A lawyer."

"Is it that obvious?" he said.

"Ivy League."

He smiled. He'd make the women on a jury swoon. "Yale," he said.

"Coincidence," I said.

"Hm?"

I patted my chest with my free hand.

"No," the lawyer said. "You're a bulldog?"

"Undergrad."

"That is so cool," he said. He slid a stool over by the bed. "That makes this whole thing more interesting to me."

"I'm glad you're interested," I said. "Why'm I shackled?"

"You're under arrest, of course."

"Why are you here?"

"That's to be determined," he said.

"Get lost."

"Listen," he said. "You are being charged with first-degree murder."

"Oh? Who? I hope it was the sheriff."

"Sheriff Cullen does have some rough edges."

"Ya think?"

"I know."

"I didn't kill anybody."

"That's to be determined."

"Quit saying that."

"You're going to be charged with killing a local named Till Felton. I understand you knew him."

"No."

"In a rather grisly fashion. He was found hanging upside down in his auto-body shop, gutted like a fish."

"Look at my face," I said.

"It's a good face," he said.

"Are you a trial lawyer?"

"On occasion."

"Can you tell when a witness is lying?"

"I'm pretty good at it."

"When I tell you I didn't kill that guy, what do you see?"

He nodded. "I never ask my clients whether they did the thing or not. I just ask about the evidence."

"I'm not your client. I have another lawyer."

"The Jew?" he said.

I let that sink in, too.

"What do you want?" I said.

"To get you out of this mess you're in," he said. "To clear you of the charge."

"In exchange for what?"

"Letting me know how much you know."

"That again?"

"Go ahead," he said. "Let me be your friend."

"We should start with the pre-socratics," I said.

"The what?"

"Greek philosophers before Socrates. Let's begin with Thales."

He stared at me a moment, then said, "I really don't

have time for this. You're in a world of hurt right now. There are any number of things that can go wrong for you. You can be tried for murder, but that's the least of it. You could have your legs amputated. Or you could disappear from the face of the earth. Or you can walk out of here no worse for wear. What'll it be?"

"We all owe God a death," I said.

"Shakespeare now?" he said.

"Yale did you some good," I said. "But they didn't teach you ethics."

"Just tell me what you know about what you know."

"I don't know," I said.

"This is pointless."

"At last we agree."

"I tried." He went to the door, paused, looked back at me. "There's a man stationed outside here. You have one hour."

"One hour for what?" I said.

He shrugged, smiled. "I don't know."

Then he went out.

G o down swinging, Moochie had said.

A little hard to do when cuffed to a side rail on a hospital bed. At least I was still in my clothes. I wasn't even sure this was a real hospital. Maybe it was some lab that removed a bruised kidney with a rusty spoon.

And they had a guard outside.

You do what you can. Better a little action against long odds than no action against any odds. A famous Greek said that—Jimmy the Greek. He was the bookmaker who famously bet on Truman to defeat Dewey. Made a lot of dough on that one.

My first action was to get out of bed and into a standing

position. I couldn't go left because of the cuff on my right
wrist. I'd have to go over the rail.

Which I did.

Not without my body protesting in pain. But I was in no
mood to hear it. I told my body to mind its own business. It
called me a bad name. I told it I'd deal with it later.

The side rail did not slide up or down. Obviously
designed for prisoners in hospital custody.

So I grabbed the top with both hands and yanked. And
bent the thing about an inch.

If there'd been a paperclip within reach, or any similar
item, I could have picked my way out of the handcuffs. Joey
Feint, the small-time PI who'd mentored me years ago in
the ways of the shamus, had taught me the fine art of
picking locks.

But the room was devoid of anything but Romeo and
the bed. There was a Formica table attached to the wall, the
kind that would have held medical tools or some such. But
it was as bare as the brain of a news anchor. A metal cabinet
above the table proved equally bereft.

It was a ridiculous scene. Me standing there with a bed
attached on one side, and a free hand on the other that had
nothing to reach for.

I suddenly thought of the book I was reading on the
plane, *Zen and the Art of Motorcycle Maintenance*. One of the
main philosophical riffs centered around the "fixing" of a
motorcycle by someone not trained in the mechanical
arts. The narrator refers to Zen Buddhism and the medi-
tative practice of "just sitting." The goal is to remove
duality—the idea of self as apart from object. So you're
not a guy over here trying to fix a problem over there.
You're part of the object, and the object is part of you.
And in that state your mind quiets down. It doesn't inter-
rupt the practice of observation and intuition. Eventually,

the answer will come. You will actually be able to fix a motorcycle.

Or get out of handcuffs without a pick?

I closed my eyes and took in a couple of deep breaths. Then I opened my eyes and simply observed. Let the answer come. Don't keep thinking there's a problem. Don't keep listing the things you can't do.

So I looked around the room. White walls. A stain on the ceiling in one corner. Water damage. This room was not cared for. It was not updated. It was instead being used for other than medical purposes. A place for someone like me to be housed. For troublemakers.

The cabinets were old. The metal handles ... if I could get one off maybe there'd be a sharp point that could manipulate the lock. But no, getting one of the handles off was not a real possibility—

Don't assess, I reminded myself. Be quiet and observe.

The formica table top was also well used. The mark of something round, like a jar, was visible in the center. The corners of the—

What was that? A slight imperfection. Part of the laminate was beginning to peel off.

Lamination. Smooth, polymeric material. Varying thickness, but if a top layer could be peeled off ... it could be hard enough to operate as a slide, which is the other way to get handcuffs off. The slide, usually metal, slips in between the opposing teeth of the interior cuff, enabling a smooth release.

Would plastic do?

Don't assess, Romeo. Just peel.

It wasn't hard at all to break off a strip of the laminated table. Now I had to see if I could peel just a bit of the top layer, the clear plastic.

At this point, natural instinct took over.

I used my teeth.

It took me a couple of minutes. But they were good, chomping minutes. I got the strip removed. It was the size of a ruler. Now I had to fashion a strip with a width small enough to slide into the cuff. And it wasn't like I had unlimited time. Somebody could come busting into that room at any moment. If they did, they'd see a foolish-looking Romeo trying to tear apart a room with his teeth.

Cool off. Don't assess. Become one with the Formica.

I couldn't believe I just thought that.

Shut up and don't think.

I used my teeth again to make a small crack at the edge of the plastic. Now it would be a matter of carefully peeling from that point down the length of the strip, fashioning a slide about a quarter of an inch wide.

It was painfully slow going. I didn't want to mess up and break it off prematurely. Then all I'd have was a long, unsanitary toothpick.

And then I was done. I had it. Now came the hard part—

The door started to open.

Timing, the old Catskills comedians used to say, is everything. Existentially, that might not be literally true. But for a good joke and an embarrassing situation, it very well holds.

Right now, I was in the latter category. Standing there with a piece of plastic in my mouth and still handcuffed to the rail of a hospital bed. My options were few.

And then came the timing. The door was open just a crack and I heard a man say, "You can get me a chicken salad on white."

My mind clicked that this was the changing of the guard and the new guy was giving his dinner order.

Which gave me just a couple of seconds to do a Fosbury Flop back onto the bed. Dick Fosbury was the high jumper who invented going over the bar on his back. It revolutionized the sport. And it saved my hide.

As I flopped over onto the bed I took the piece of plastic out of my mouth with my free hand and put it under my butt.

The bed creaked and my bracelets jangled. I made a pretense of pulling on the rail as if I were trying to get loose.

Which brought the new man into the room. He was big and ugly and wore a gray suit with a white shirt and no tie.

"Hey," he said with no charm, "cut it out."

I stopped and stared at him. "Let me out of this or the law'll be coming down on you."

That made him snort. He had a piggish nose which made the sound absurd.

"I just want to make sure you're as comfortable as possible," he said. "You gotta pee or anything? I got a plastic jug outside."

"Of course I need to pee," I said.

He left and I listened. I heard some talking and then the new guy express some sort of farewell. A moment later he came back in with one of those hospital portables into which the bed-ridden relieve themselves. He tossed it to me.

"Don't miss," he said. "I'm not cleaning anything up."

"Unlock me," I said.

"Come on, sport," he said.

"How long am I going to be here?"

"Not my call. Just do your thing and be a good boy. I

don't want to have to come in here and readjust things, like your face."

"That's big talk to a guy who's chained to a bed. Why don't you unlock me and you and I can have our own one-on-one?"

"Yeah, right. Just shut up and pee."

He let the door close and I was alone again.

I recovered the bit of plastic from under my patoot then went back to work. It wasn't pretty, but I finally had my last hope in my fingertips. The only slide I ever practiced with, courtesy of Joey Feint, was thin and bendable metal. No such luxury now.

The real trick as you push in the slide is to close the handcuff a click or two tighter. This moves the teeth but the slide then keeps them from engaging.

Once again, timing is everything. It had been over ten years since I'd done this.

I held the cuff against my chest and the slide between my left thumb and index finger. The other fingers I used to press the cuff down for that all-important click.

A bead of sweat actually trickled down my forehead and into my eye. It was a movie moment. Give me a closeup here, camera guy.

Click.

Push.

And then I was free.

I wiped the sweat off me with the back of my hand. I got out of the bed and did the same release trick with the other cuff.

Then I put the cuffs together and laced the fingers of my right hand through them both.

Giving me iron knuckles.

I almost hated to do this to the poor sap outside the door. But only almost.

I screamed, "Help!"

H e came blasting in. On his face, for a brief moment, was an expression of rage. Just before the blow that was to end his day, he turned and saw me and his eyes changed. There was that brief reflection of the thought *What the* —

—as my fist smashed his nose into cartilage putty.

He was out before he hit the floor. For good measure, his head thudded on the hard surface of the floor.

Blood poured out of his shattered proboscis.

I dragged him fully into the room and handcuffed him to the bed rail. There was a bulge at his right hip. I pulled up his shirt and saw a leather conceal-carry holster. I pulled out the gun. A Heckler and Koch VP9. I pulled the slide far enough to see there was a round in the pipe. I unclipped his holster and put the gun back in and slid the combo into my waistband.

Outside the door was what looked like an office that had lost its lease. Next to the door was a folding chair, a crumpled bag, and a coffee mug.

The lights were on. There was one window with closed blinds. I went over and peeked out. I was on the first floor of the building. A parking lot with several cars in a narrow row stretched out to the right. To the left was desert.

In front was the hospital. In daylight. Late morning, it looked like.

And in the room one Mike Romeo, who had no idea how to get away from this place.

Run?

Where?

And with what? My leg wasn't fully recovered, and half my torso felt like it was stepped on by an elephant.

A car would be nice. Sure, just somebody give me your keys, thank you, have a nice day.

Or, since I had a gun, carjack some poor guy.

What a citizen.

B ut first I had to get out of the room and find an exit without being seen.

This was going to be fun.

I opened the door a crack and looked out. A hallway stretched to a corridor that went to the right. Poking my head out, I scanned the opposite direction. The hallway ended at a set of double doors. Calculating what I knew from the window view, I figured that led further into the hospital.

If this were a movie, I would be able to locate a set of hospital scrubs and could walk around as if I belonged.

Not a movie.

I ducked out to the right. Went down to the end of the corridor where there was another right turn. Just as I got there I heard women's voices coming toward me. But from where? There were double doors to my left. To my right was a restroom sign. I went into the alcove and pushed the men's room door. Locked. A little round sign read *Occupied*. Having no other choice, and this being a new age anyway, I went into the women's restroom. There were four stalls. I took the one at the end and closed the door.

The two women came in, still talking. They were speaking Spanish. I didn't catch much of it. I got the word for *Tuesday* and the word for *work*. Apparently, the women did not like either. I heard a stall door open and close and latch. Running water came from a sink. The women spoke some more. I picked up the word for *fat* and the word for *chicken*. I did not sense there was a relationship between the two.

After a minute came the sound of a flushing toilet, an unlatched and opened stall door. More water from the sink. More talking between the women. And then the talk faded as they left.

After a beat, I got out of the stall and went to the door and peeked out. The sign on the men's room now said *Vacant*.

Out I went and continued toward the exit. I got there without further incident. Which wasn't a major victory, because now I was outside in the bright sun, with no means of getting anywhere except on foot.

I wondered where Moochie was. Still in jail? Or did they ferry him off somewhere, too?

What if I just walked to town? I figured not many people knew of a secret room where certain people kept certain other people incommunicado. On the other hand, there had to be more than one or two who were part of the operation. If they saw Mike Romeo walking free as a bird toward town, they'd call out the cavalry.

What about the old back of the truck routine? You know, where a convict jumps on the back of a laundry truck heading out of the gates.

I saw no trucks.

Plan B, make a beeline for the desert.

That didn't work so well last time.

Plan C ...

There was no plan C.

I looked around, no people in the parking lot. Maybe a dozen cars. Toward the front of the hospital a car pulled in and stopped. A young man got out, went around, opened the door and helped an old woman out.

Steal the car?

Such thoughts come to you unbidden when you're on the run.

As I was standing there like a lizard on an exposed rock, a golf cart came around the corner and puttered toward me. On the front of the golf cart it said, *Security*.

The gun was in my waistband, in the back.

I fiddled with the top button of my shirt.

The security guard was male, black, wore shades and a baseball cap that went with his uniform. He made no move to speak into his shoulder mic. That was a good sign. I smiled and gave him a friendly nod.

He did not return the gesture. He pulled to a stop.

"Help you?" he said.

"I'm good," I said.

"Can I ask what you're doing back here?"

"Waiting," I said. "My ride's coming."

He looked me over.

"You sure?" he said.

"Absolutely," I said.

"All right. Have a nice day."

"You, too."

He rolled on but left a lingering doubt behind him. I was sure he was going to circle slowly around and keep an eye on me. Or maybe call somebody else to help check on me.

Either way I had to get out of there. They'd be checking on me inside. Maybe they were there now. The prison break sirens would be blaring soon.

Had to be the desert. If I could make it a mile or so, I could bank left and get into town and maybe hole up at Biff's, make a call, get Ira and the FBI down here to sort this all out.

If no one came gunning for me, that is.

I started walking through the parking lot. My body was creaky. Muscles were bunched up in my back.

Then I saw the fence.

Why hadn't I noticed it before? It was chain link and went all the way around the parking lot.

For a moment I just stopped and stared at it, like a lab rat. Which way to the freaking cheese? It was like one of those nightmares where you keep trying to get somewhere but can't. Each door, each path, leads to some further aspect of loss. And then strange things happen...

...like a black sedan with heavily tinted windows speeding right at me.

A reflex is an involuntary action your body takes in response to a distress signal from the brain. The entire transaction takes place in the blink of an eye which is itself a reflex. When the muscles receive the message from the brain, they spring into immediate action. To the extent they can. If they've been beaten down or injured, they may attempt a move they may be unable to complete with success. Like the guy with the mediocre voice who comes to every Karaoke night and tries to belt out "My Way" like Sinatra.

For me, to keep from becoming grill kill, my body wanted to jump right, ball up, and roll. But my left leg was still in recovery. It did its best, but only managed half the force it needed. It got me above the grill, but not far enough away that half my body slammed against the windshield.

From there, it was tumbling tumbleweed time. From what I can remember, my head hit the asphalt first. A light show went off behind my eyes then quickly faded to a dull shadow. I remember thinking *Gun* but my arms did not respond.

Then it was like a giant octopus was on me, a monster from a sci-fi undersea adventure. And while I tried to fight back, my strength was gone. The tentacles squeezed and pulled and lifted and shoved. When the crashing metallic junk in my brain finally quieted down I was in the back of the car with my arms behind me. What felt like zip ties cut into my wrists. My left leg—my poor, abused, left-side wheel—was throbbing with fresh pain. I was on my side and a hand the size of a ham was pushing my head into the seat. What felt like a gun was jammed against my brain stem.

I thought about saying something sharp and witty to my captors, but just didn't have the energy for it. For certain, I was not going to be writing tourist brochures for Dillard any time soon.

A fter what seemed a mile or so the sedan slowed, then stopped. What light there was suddenly cut off. Like a garage door had closed.

Which, when I was finally let up, was exactly what had happened.

Now I could see who the driver was. Gus Deveroes. He stood quietly outside the car as the two sides of beef pulled me out and shoved me through the door that led into a house. I didn't have time to see much of it. They took me to a doorway that had stairs and gave me a healthy shove. My reflexes went into action and this time served me well. I tap danced like Fred Astaire down the steps, managing to keep my balance.

At the bottom was nothing but a cement box. Some-body had gone to a lot of trouble for this little bunker. Houses out west don't usually have cellars, especially in the desert. This one was not a place for fine wines. It was a place for private imprisonment.

The door to the stairwell shut, and I was alone in the dark.

Just to be sociable, I felt around the box with my shoulder and feet. It was about ten by ten. Less than a standard jail cell. It didn't have the amenities of a cell. No sink or toilet. A good place to ride out the nuclear apocalypse.

Which would be welcome right about now. Whether it was produced by God or nature, mankind had grossly overstayed its welcome. The trend line was not exactly on the upswing. Most ancient religions have predictions to this effect. An Assyrian tablet from 2800 B.C. points to society in moral deterioration requiring destruction. The Bible, of course, has The Book of Revelation. In Norse mythology, there's the Ragnarok, where giants of frost and fire fight the gods in a final battle that will ultimately destroy the planet, submerging it under water. Beats the bomb, I guess.

Even as dark thoughts crowded me in the dark chamber, that little spark of fight flickered in my chest. Maybe we're going down, yes, but we don't have to go quietly. Moochie had it right. Go down swinging.

But how could I swing when my arms were zip-tied behind my back? When I had no way of getting out of this place? When somebody with a gun would open the door and come down to finish the job?

Which hadn't been finished. Why?

I sat on the bottom step. Not knowing how long I was going to be there, I started my review of Western philosophy, beginning with Augustine, traipsing through John Scotus Eriugena and Anselm, and spending a good bit of time—an hour maybe?—with Aquinas. It was when I started on Descartes that the door at the top of the stairs opened and a little bit of light spilled in.

A low wattage light bulb clicked on above me. Two guys came down the stairs, one carrying a chair, the other carrying a machine pistol of the Uzi variety. And some rope.

"The night crew?" I said.

They said nothing. They were big and dressed in black tracksuits. I thought I recognized one of the faces. Probably the same two who had me in the back of the car.

The one guy put the chair down in the middle of the box, then pulled me up and sat me on it. The other guy put the gun to my forehead. The first guy ripped my shirt off.

"Now you have to take me out to dinner," I said.

Still no smiles from my captive audience. Shirt Ripper then took the rope from the gun guy and proceeded to tie me nice and snug to the chair.

Gun Guy removed the gun from my head and the two started up the stairs.

"Next time you drop in," I said, "bring your folks."

The light went off and the door slammed.

They let me think about it for awhile. Taking their time. Ira once told me about interrogation techniques, one of which he called pulse pounding. I told him that sounded like a blurb for an action movie. He explained it was a way to keep a prisoner's pulse going up and down and back up by making him wait...and wait. It was almost as effective as the rubber hose.

All this before he was a rabbi, you understand.

So I breathed in and out, steadily, and picked up my review of philosophy with Hobbes. There was a man after my own heart. In the 1600s he managed to tick off every political party in Britain and had to flee for his life. His philosophy was pessimistic. He said that life was "nasty, brutish, and short," and that the only motive anyone had—

because it was ingrained—is the quest for power. We eat each other up if we can.

At the moment, I couldn't think of a good argument against that.

Spinoza was next, and then Leibniz. Maybe another hour gone by. Then the door opened again, the light went on, and two new people came down the stairs.

They were new because they were not big like the other two, they wore simple clothes—jeans and sweatshirts—and had ski masks over their heads.

The one in front carried a long rod. The one in back had a bucket in one hand and a duffel bag in the other.

"Really?" I said. "Ski masks? Not very original."

The guy with the rod said, "We know all about your mouth, Mike. You can use it to save yourself a lot of pain. You know what this is?"

He held up the prod.

"Broken bicycle seat," I said.

"It's a picana. You heard of that?"

"A type of blanched nut?" I said.

"If only," he said. "This delivers high voltage at a low current. It's used for torture quite a bit in the Middle East. They're good at that sort of thing."

He made a motion to the other guy, who put the bucket and duffel bag down. He unzipped the duffel and pulled out a box with some controls on it. And then a car battery.

The first guy started connecting wires to the rod. "Now we know you're a strong guy, a brave guy, but why go through all this? Just tell us who you're working for and we won't even go the first step."

"I work out of LA, for a lawyer," I said. "I came to Nevada to interview a witness. I was on the plane that went down outside of this town, which I find the most inhospitable place on the face of the earth. I'd like to leave now, and thanks for your good wishes."

"You're not here because of the Jew lawyer. That's not why you came back. You showed an unusual interest in someone who was on the plane with you, and in the hospital, and in the sheriff's station. You went to Las Vegas and had a run-in with someone over, what was it, Chinese food? This resulted in an unfortunate death. Yet now here you are again. We want to know how all this fits together."

"Coincidence," I said.

The guy shook his masked head. He gave a nod to the other guy. That guy put his hand in the bucket and came out with a big, sloppy sponge. He squeezed the water all over my chest.

The first guy said, "This is just to give you a taste."

He shoved the prod in my side.

And zapped.

My body went stiff. Fire hit every nerve.

Oh yeah, he knew what he was doing.

"So let's revisit in a little while," he said. He put the box and battery and prod into the duffel bag, and started up the stairs. Bucket Guy followed.

Pulse pounding.

It worked. My pulse went ballistic.

M ore waiting. I was now up to Locke. Then Berkeley, who sought to prove that only minds and ideas exist, not bodies. At that moment, I wished he was right. But my own body told me Berkeley was full of ... beans.

Beans...Pinto beans. What happened to Noah? Too many questions for me to give up now.

Zip ties, tight. Rope around me, tight. The guy who did it knew his knots.

Minds exist. Ideas exist. Bodies exist.

Who's next?

Hume. The skeptic. I didn't have time for Hume.

The stairwell door opened.

A flashlight beamed.

Down the steps it came. The light bounced off the wall and illuminated something in the guy's hand.

A knife.

A big one. Eight-inch blade at least.

So this was how it would end.

"Do I get a last request?" I said.

The beam paused at the foot of the stairs.

I said, "My request is I'd like to read *Lord of the Rings* again."

The flashlight and the beam came forward.

Then went around in back.

A second later the zip ties were cut off me. Then the ropes.

"You need to get out now," the voice said.

It was a woman's voice, one I knew.

"Karen?" I said.

"Hurry," she said.

"What is this?" I said. "How are—"

"You have only a few minutes."

I stood. "Why are you here?"

"No time," she said. "Wait one minute then go up the stairs and out of the house the way you came in. The garage door is open."

"Why are you doing this? Who are these people?"

She started to turn but I grabbed her shoulders.

"Are you all right?" I said.

"Please go," she said.

"Just tell me you're all right."

"I will be," she said. "Hurry."

She broke out of my hold and ran back up the stairs. The whole thing was nuts, but I wasn't in any position to hang around. Whatever this all meant, she'd given me one shot at getting away.

And I took it. I went up the stairs, opened the door, listened, heard nothing. I went to the door to the garage, opened it. The garage door was indeed open. It was a clear night and starry sky. And Mike Romeo was on the run.

Literally. Shirtless, but able to hoof it down the only road to the house behind me. There was plenty of land between it and the next house, which was dark. I knew I was running in the general direction of Dillard.

My legs were doing remarkably well for what they'd been through. Adrenaline is a wonderful thing.

After a half a mile or so I banked right, seeing the lights of Dillard, such as they were. What time was it? It felt like midnight. My body felt like midnight. The whole world felt like midnight. The thought pounding in my head was, why was Karen Morrison in that house?

All this time I'd been trying to find her. Then the moment she finds me, I can't talk to her.

Where was I going? I thought about trying to find my way to Moochie's house, but I wasn't sure where or how far. I had to get to a phone. The only place where that might be possible at this hour was Biff's.

Not wanting to be seen on the main street, I cut to the back. I heard music inside. But the back door was locked.

I pounded.

Nothing.

Pounded again.

The door opened. A big guy in a flannel shirt was there, zipping up his pants. Behind him was a door marked MEN.

"What's up with you?" he said.

"Thanks," I said, and stepped past him.

"Hey," he said. "No shirt, no service." Then he laughed.

I walked into the bar. Half a dozen people there, three at the bar. The bartender was the same mortician-looking fellow. When he saw me his eyes about popped.

He said, "Hey!"

At the edge of the bar I said, "I need to use your phone."

"Use your own," he said.

"Don't have one."

"Why don't you got a shirt on?"

"Can I use your phone?"

"You shouldn't be here."

"Phone!"

One of the men at the bar, a sour-looking souse, pointed at me. "You heard the man. Get out."

Now what? I could go behind the bar and take the phone by force. But there'd be a tussle about it, and the bartender no doubt had access to some fire power.

"I knew you'd come back."

I turned. It was Candy Sumner.

"Use my phone," she said.

"Thanks," I said.

"Come outside." She started for the back door.

I followed. She went out, I went out, and she kept walking.

"Where you going?" I said.

She just motioned at me to keep following. There was a yellow Volkswagen bug at the end of the lot. At least I think it was yellow. A veneer of dirt and dust made it hard to say for sure.

"Get in," she said.

"Look, all I need is—"

"You need to come with me," she said.

I felt like giving a primal scream at the universe.

"Do you have a phone on you?" I said.

"No."

"Then what—"

"You'll understand."

She got in and started the bug. Reluctantly, I got in, too.

As she pulled out of the lot, she said, "Remember I told you everything has a reason and a season? Remember that?"

"Yes."

"This is it. This is everything coming together. You coming here tonight confirms it."

"Confirms what?"

"You'll see."

"Why don't you just tell me?"

She shook her head. "This season is Candy's season. I been waiting for it a long time."

The faint smell of beer breath in the car told me it wasn't much of a life. But then again, what did I have to show for mine? I was still looking for my reason and season.

"Can you tell me where we're going?" I said.

"My place," she said. Then added, "Don't worry. I got no designs. I got something better. I know what you been up to."

"Do tell."

"Uh-uh. I want this just the way I want it."

"You do have a phone at your place, right?"

"Oh yeah. You'll get your phone. And a whole lot more."

I gulped.

"All my life people been thinking low of me," Candy said as the bug sputtered on. "Ever since I was a little girl and didn't do so good on the spelling bee. Mama said some just got more brain power than others, and I was one of them others, and had to learn to live with it. You know what I'm talking about?"

"I do," I said.

"Well, I'm through livin' with it."

"That's good."

"Is it?" she said.

"It's a decision," I said. "All good things start with a decision."

She turned onto a dirt road. "My place isn't much. Don't laugh, okay?"

"I won't laugh," I said.

"It's just an old ramshackle my Mama left me when she died."

" 'Tis shelter from the stormy blast."

"Huh?"

"It's good to have a roof over your head."

"Yeah. Boy, you say the craziest things."

"So I've been told."

Then we were at the house, sitting all by itself at the end of the road. In the headlights it looked like a place where criminals in an old B movie would hole up.

The inside did not look as messy as it did neglected. There was an old throw rug on the wooden floor, and a little table on the rug. The table had some papers and a dish and a stack of DVDs. A red chair was against the wall and some clothes on it. Leaning against the chair was a broom, and next to the broom, on the floor, was a Windex spray bottle. On the other side of the table was a brown sofa. It only had a pillow on it.

"I need coffee," Candy said. "Can I make you some?"

"Phone first," I said.

"Who you need to call?"

"Some help."

"It's about this thing you're working on, isn't it?" She was playing it coy. Not what I needed at the moment.

"Candy, will you please lay it all out for me? Why am I here?"

Tossing me a smile, she turned and went into the kitchen. I followed. She flicked on the light. The kitchen was a match for the living room, except it was dishes and silverware instead of clothes and papers all around.

She moved slowly, like she wanted to drag out the moment. And started humming. She waltzed over to the sink. Then she looked back at me and smiled as she reached up, without looking, and opened a cupboard. She took out a round tin and set it on the counter by the sink. After another dramatic pause and smile, she reached in and pulled out my digital recorder. She held it on her palm and said, "How do you like them apples?"

I took it from her, looked at it. "How?"

"I was there. I saw you do it."

"At the Longbranch?"

She nodded.

"Why?" I said.

"To show you."

"Show me what?"

"To show everybody," she said.

I waited.

She said, "That I matter. That I can do things. I sat in the corner and watched you stick it under the table. When Cullen and Gus left, I went over and took it."

"Did you listen to it?"

"I think you're going to be very interested," she said.

"I'll take that coffee now," I said.

As Candy made the joe I went back to the living room and listened to the recording. It was killer. There was mention of accounting practices at the hospital, the Eurasians putting pressure on Deveroes, and, according to Cullen, how Mike Romeo had to be eliminated because he was probably working with the FBI.

By the time she came in with the coffee, I was ready to roll.

"Phone?"

"Over there."

She pointed to a corded phone sitting on the floor by the red chair. I was never so happy to see a hunk of retro technology in my life.

I grabbed the handset and put it to my ear.

Nothing.

I hit the plunger a couple of times.

Dead air.

"It doesn't work," I said.

"What?" Candy came over and took the handset from me. "It did this morning."

Instinct. I jumped on Candy and took her down as a blast shattered her front window.

"Stay down!" I said, pushing off her and diving toward the wall.

A second blast shattered more glass and part of the wall that barely protected me.

Every indication—sound, shatter pattern, aftermath—cried shotgun. Meant to hit but also freeze us. The next move would be somebody through the door, weapon ready.

How many there were I couldn't tell, but I had no time to assess.

As we sat there in a lighted room.

The light was coming from a table lamp on the far side. And the kitchen. Which I could reach with partial covering from the wall. I jumped up and flicked off the light, and grabbed a kitchen chair. I spun out of the kitchen and threw the chair like a soccer ball across the room, over Candy, and into the lamp.

Candy yelped and the house went dark.

"Sh!" I said, and three-stepped to the other side of the room, just as the front door crashed open.

A flashlight beam followed.

I aimed my kick a foot above the beam. It was beautiful. To the face. The guy went down. As soon as he hit the ground I took the shotgun from him and gave him a gun-butt to the face. He would not be getting up anytime soon.

The flashlight was on the floor. It was a heavy Maglite. I took and shined it at the guy.

It was Deputy Sam.

Second instinct. I tossed the light and ducked as automatic gunfire sprayed over my head.

A figure came through the door and started emptying his gun at the flashlight.

I fired. The guy in the door folded over and went down.

I pumped the shotgun and got ready for the next guy.

There was no next guy. It took me a minute to verify that, and also that the dead man was Sheriff Les Cullen.

"What's happening?" Candy said.

"Sit tight," I said.

"Are we all right?"

"For now."

Deputy Sam groaned. I took his sidearm, then patted him down and got his phone.

I had to borrow Sam's thumb to unlock it. He didn't resist.

Ira picked up after the fourth ring.

"Michael, what is it?"

"A whole lot. I got the recording—"

"How?"

"Just listen. It's got what we need. But I've also got two bodies here, one that's still moving."

"Oh no."

"The dead guy is the sheriff, Cullen."

"Oh dear."

"They tried to kill me. I've got a witness. There's more. But you need to get down here with Agent Ramos and however many she can bring with her."

"It's late...early."

"Do what you have to do, but make it fast."

"Where are you?"

"Can you track this phone?"

"Hold on." Pause. "Got it."

"Hurry."

I gathered the firepower—two automatic pistols, one from each, and the pump-action shotgun. I dragged Cullen's body outside to the front porch.

Inside it was still dark, except for the flashlight, which was enough at the moment.

Candy was crying. I went to her. She was curled up in a ball. I lifted her and pulled her to my chest.

"It's over," I whispered. "Hang in there for me."

She kept crying.

I held her tighter. "I need you to be calm. We've got to be ready for anything."

She caught her breath and managed to say, "What...does that mean?"

"There are other deputies. They may be stopping by. And..."

"And what?"

"Just hold on for me. Help is on the way."

Deputy Sam moaned.

"Will you be okay for me?" I said.

"Yes," Candy said.

"Good."

I went over to Sam. Even in the dim light I could tell one side of his face was swollen and bloody. He looked up at me and said something. It rhymed with duck.

"It's over, Sam," I said.

He said the same word and added a personal pronoun.

"Sorry to hear that," I said. With no gentle intent I grabbed his shirt and flipped his body over. The puffy side of his face hit the floor. He cried out. I took the cuffs off his belt and shackled his arms behind his back. I got the red chair and put it on top of him. My one act of mercy was not sitting in it.

Candy said, "What are you going to do to him?"

"Deputy Sam? Educate him."

"Huh?"

"I'm a teacher at heart, I guess," I said.

Sam moaned.

I said, "In an investigation of this magnitude, with the FBI involved, there's a little something called the federal death penalty in play. Sam here was involved in a felony, which you have witnessed. There's a sheriff outside who is quite dead."

"But you ..."

"Self-defense," I said. "Perfectly justified. But because the death came about during the commission of a felonious and violent activity, the felony-murder rule applies."

"What's that?"

"When a bad man, such as Sam here, is in the process of committing a violent felony, like murder, and someone else is killed, like his partner in crime, then he is going to be held to have murdered his own partner."

"That's wild," Candy said.

"That's common law," I said.

Sam was silent.

And it was within that silence that I heard an approaching car.

I grabbed the flashlight and turned it off. Taking Candy by the arm, I sat her in the chair on top of Deputy Sam. He went *Oof.* The chair leaned against the wall.

"If he makes a sound," I said, "hit him in the face with this." I put the Maglite in her hand.

Then I gathered up the guns and took them out the back door.

T he car was another sheriff's vehicle. It pulled up behind the other and stopped. From the side of the house I watched as one deputy emerged. When he stepped in front of his headlights, I could tell it was the one called Rand. He paused and looked at the first vehicle, then at the dark house.

He had his own Maglite. And that was trouble. He'd see Cullen's body. And probably pull his gun.

Surprise was my only choice.

Twenty-five yards was what I had to cover. I could do that in four or five seconds. A twitchy deputy might be able to pull a sidearm in that time. So I added an abdominal *kiai* to my dash. *Kiai* is the ancient art of screaming, to freeze your opponent and focus your fighting energy. It comes from the gut, not the throat. It impacts the opponent's nervous system, rattling it for a couple of seconds.

Deputy Rand didn't even raise his flashlight, so frozen was he.

I jumped the last two yards and came down with my arm around his throat.

"Easy, Rand," I said, reaching around with my free hand and removing his gun. I tossed it aside. "I don't know how much you know, but you may not be involved. Then again, you may be up to your ears in it. We're going to find out soon. Take off your duty belt."

He hesitated, then unbuckled his Sam Browne. It fell to the ground.

"Now keys and phone," I said.

Rand retrieved both. I put his phone in my pocket and keeping hold of his neck walked him over to his squad car.

"I'm going to lock you in back, just like an arrestee. Anyone else know you're here?"

He shook his head.

"If you lie about this, you may end up dead," I said. "Are you sure?"

He nodded.

"In you go."

I locked him in.

Back inside I said, "How's it going?"

"He hasn't made a move," Candy said.

"I *can't* make a move," Sam said. "Let me up."

"Tell me where Moochie Harrison is."

"Jail," he said.

"I'm so tired," Candy said.

"Let me up," Sam said.

I chambered a round in Rand's semi-auto. It was a Beretta M9. I took the Maglite from Candy and shined the light on the gun.

"See that red dot?" I said.

"Yes," Candy said.

"That means the gun is live, it's ready to shoot. Keep your finger off the trigger. If Sam here tries to do anything put your left hand under your right hand, like this. Then aim at his chest and pull the trigger. You can shoot him several times. Make sense?"

"Yes."

"Let's sit you over here." I took her to the sofa and set up the Maglite so it was on Sam. "Can I depend on you not to let him sweet talk you into anything?"

"For sure," Candy said.

"If he tries, shoot him in the leg."

"Come on!" Sam said.

"Where are you going?" Candy said.

"I'll be back," I said.

I hoped I would be.

O utside, I went to Rand's vehicle and opened the trunk. The light showed me a pump-action shotgun. I picked it up, opened the action, took out the first round. The second round popped out on the shell elevator, ready to be chambered. I took that shell out and rolled the gun on its side, then pushed the elevator down. Pinching the shell latch on the left side I took out three more shells. Good. I reloaded and got in the front seat.

"What are you doing?" Rand said.

"I suggest you lie down back there," I said. "Things may get a little rough."

"Wait. What?"

As I drove the cruiser back toward the Karen Morrison house, I said, "How much do you know about the Eurasians?"

"The who?"

"Don't pretend with me, Rand. Cullen is dead."

No answer.

"Did you hear me?" I said.

"You killed him?"

"Uh-huh. But in all fairness, he was going to kill me."

Rand swore.

"So how much do you know?" I said.

"About who again?"

"Eurasians. Medical fraud. The hospital. Cullen."

"I don't ... I don't...." He sounded genuinely confused.

"If you don't talk now, it'll be worse for you when the feds take you in."

"Feds?"

"You know, FBI?"

"What is going on?"

"The house up ahead, the blue one on the little hill. You know it?"

"What house?"

"The only one out this way."

"Where are we?"

"It's where Gus Deveroes and his boys brought me."

"Deveroes," Rand said.

"Yeah."

"I don't trust him."

"Good call," I said. "Do you know about this house or not?"

"Which house again?"

I cut the headlights as I drove by. "The only one here."

Rand peered out the window. "I think that belongs to a lawyer. I don't know his name."

"Never been inside?"

"No, never."

"Okay, you'll need to stay down in case there's any shooting."

"What!"

"Sh."

I made a U-turn and headed back to the house. I took the shotgun and one of the nines, and got out.

"Don't let them see you," I said.

"Who see me?"

"Whoever comes out that door."

"Wait!"

I didn't wait. I reached in and turned on the emergency lights. The night filled with red and blue flashes.

I t took about thirty seconds for one of the big beefs to come out. I was crouching at the back of the car, street side.

"Hey," the beef called out. "What's up?"

Closer.

"Cullen?"

He reached the car and bent over to look in the window. He even put his hands on it, nicely shielding his eyes from me coming around the cruiser.

He looked up just before I gave the back of his head the shotgun-butt treatment. Down he went. I checked him for weapons. All he had was a knife. I put that in my waistband next to the pistol.

I unlocked the rear door of the cruiser.

"Look out," I said.

"Who is that?" Rand said.

"Seat mate." I pulled the hulk up by his shirt, bent him over, and shoved him in. His head fell into Rand's lap.

"Hey!" Rand said.

I closed the door and headed up the small hill to the front of the house.

The door was open.

The living room was dark. There was light coming from a room down the hall. I heard what sounded like a sitcom—canned audience laughter every five seconds.

I waited, listened. Picked up no movement or activity in the front part of the house.

Then down the hall, slowly, toward the room with the light. As I came to the door I saw a big guy lying on a bed, hands laced behind his head, eyes on the TV. He was laughing.

The laughter stopped when he saw me and the shotgun.

He sat up.

"Don't move," I said. "Let me see your hands."

Slowly, he put his hands up to shoulder level.

"Where is she?" I said.

He just glared.

"Stand up," I said. "I'm going to shoot your knees."

"What?"

"Up. I want to blast your knees."

"Wh ... why?"

"Because you're not answering my question. I'll shoot your knees, ask you again, and if you don't answer I'll shoot something else. Or, you can tell me now."

He said nothing.

"Stand up," I said.

He didn't move. The little flat screen TV was still playing the sitcom. I blasted it with the shotgun. The guy went "Ah!" The TV went dead.

"Last chance," I said.

"The basement," he said. "Where you were."

"She tied up?"

"Where's my brother?"

"I'll take you to him."

"You will?" he said.

"If you cooperate," I said.

"Don't shoot me," he said.

"Don't make me wait," I said.

Hands in the air, he got off the bed. I backed out of the

room, the business end of the shotgun pointed at his mass, which was plenty.

In the hallway I said, "Hold it. You carrying?"

"No."

"I'm going to pat you down," I said. "If I find any weapon I will shoot your knees."

Pause. "Okay. A knife."

"Toss it on the floor."

He had it in a hidden sheath. He threw it on the floor between us.

"Where's the guy with the picana?" I said.

"The what?"

"Knees." I lowered the barrel to his legs.

"Okay, he's gone."

"He coming back?"

"I don't know! What are you gonna do?"

"Down we go."

H e opened the door to the basement and down we went. The light on.

Karen was tied up in the same chair she'd freed me from.

"Thank God," she said.

"You all right?" I said.

"Not really."

"Untie her," I told the beef.

He did as instructed. Karen got up and came to the stairs where I was.

"Now what?" Beef said.

"Easiest thing would be to kill you," I said.

"Come on, man," he said.

I said to Karen, "What do you suggest?"

"No, don't," she said.

"Sit in the chair," I said.

He paused, then sat.

I said, "Take that piece of rope and tie your legs together, good and tight, above the knees."

"What about my brother?" he said.

"I made you a promise," I said. "But first you tie your legs. If it's not tight, I shoot your knees."

"Stop saying that!" He picked up a piece of rope and did a good job on his legs.

"Now stand up and put your hands behind you," I said.

He did.

To Karen I said, "Go tie his wrists as tightly as you can."

Karen picked up another piece of rope and stepped behind Beef.

"You don't need to do this, Karen," Beef said.

"You have nothing to say to me," Karen said.

I smiled. There was a tough nut under that demure shell.

When she was done I grabbed Beef by the back of the shirt and put the barrel of the shotgun on his neck. I waddled him to the stairs. He was like a toddler learning to walk. Step by step, we got to the top.

I guided him down to the sheriff's car, Karen behind us. The bloody face of his brother looked out the window at us.

"There he is," I said.

I took Beef to the back of the vehicle, unlocked the trunk and sat him on the edge.

"What are you gonna do to me?" he said.

"*Forsan et haec olim meminisse iuvabit*," I said.

"Huh?"

"Perhaps this will be a pleasure to look back on someday."

Then I hit him in the head with the butt of the shotgun.

I was getting rather good at that.

He fell into the trunk. I shut it.

Everybody was quiet on the ride back to Candy's house. I left the prisoners in the car and took Karen inside with me. Candy was on the sofa, gun in hand.

"How's our boy doing?" I said.

"I want to talk!" Sam said. "I want to make a deal!"

I said, "Gotta tell you, Sam, your idea of a negotiating position leaves a lot to be desired."

A n hour later Ira and the FBI arrived. Ira in his van, the feds in two black SUVs. Agent Ramos had three other agents with her.

It took some time to sort things out, clear the trunk, rearrange the players. But by the time morning light hit Dillard, Nevada, Agent Ramos was driving me to the Dillard jail.

In the car I said, "This should make you happy." I put the digital recorder on the dash.

"I have a feeling it's going to take some sweet legal talk to use that," she said.

"You'll figure out a way," I said. "At the very least you can use it as leverage to get Deveroes to talk. Too bad about Cullen."

"What was it Oliver Hardy used to say? Another nice mess?"

"You rate high on cultural literacy," I said.

At the jail we found a tired and nervous woman deputy. Dunlap. I remembered her name from the first time I'd seen her here. Agent Ramos flashed credentials and explained a few things. Dunlap got Moochie out of the can.

He was spitting Old West epithets when he came into the front office.

I calmed him as best I could. "You've got to get home and take care of Bill," I said.

Moochie grumbled, then said, "Anybody find out what happened to Noah?"

"Not yet," I said. "But if anybody can sweat it out of Deputy Sam, it's Agent Damita Ramos.

She pretended she didn't hear me.

I t took another week before Ira and I got out of Las Vegas. When it all shook out, Deputy Sam sang like a meadowlark in order to avoid a possible death penalty. His song included tapping Cullen for the murder of Till Felton, who had been making noises about getting more money or singing himself.

The United States Attorney's Office was in negotiations with Sally Hoskin for her testimony in return for a grant of immunity.

Candy Sumner decided she'd had enough of Dillard, and planned to stay with her sister in Elko for awhile.

And then there was Karen Morrison. She had quite a tale to tell. Agent Ramos was good enough to let me hear it live and in person as the three of us sat in an FBI conference room together.

Turns out Karen was the wife of the lawyer type who questioned me in the hospital, right before I broke out and got whammed by the car driven by Gus Deveroes. Said lawyer, Caleb Morrison, was part of the layer of protection for the Eurasian network that stretched from Nevada through Kansas all the way to the East Coast.

Karen was in the dark about all that. But she began to sense her husband was afraid of something, or under great stress for some reason. He sloughed off the suggestions.

Then he became increasingly distant and angry, so much so Karen contemplated leaving him.

He beat her to it. He left one day without a word. Would not answer his phone. Karen couldn't shake the suspicion that Caleb was being threatened by some criminal—a former client perhaps?—or a criminal enterprise. And she'd once overheard him talking about bad things happening in Las Vegas.

Karen got her ticket to Vegas the next day. It was her intent to go to the FBI and see if they could help locate her husband. Or help her figure out what might be going on with him.

Then the plane went down.

When the guy in the Ram Power Wagon came by to take Karen into Dillard, I'd made sure to tell him to go to the hospital.

"And that's where they took me," Karen said. "They checked me in, and I was put in an observation room for a time. Until a man—not a doctor—came in and asked me if I was Caleb Morrison's wife."

"That was Gus Deveroes," Agent Ramos said to me. "We have him in the lockup."

"And where is Caleb?" I said.

"We've got him," said Agent Ramos. "Nabbed him at the airport."

Karen sighed and for a moment looked lost. Then she took a deep breath and continued. "Shortly after that I was taken out of the room and put in a car and driven to a house, the one where I cut you loose. They held me there as a virtual prisoner. They didn't trust me. I told them I'd only come out here to try to find my husband. Caleb wasn't buying it. Then when they got you and brought you to the house, Caleb said I could prove myself."

"How?" I said.

"By helping him with the ... whatever that thing was."

"Cattle prod will do," I said.

"I didn't want that to happen."

"I appreciate it," I said. "But how were you able to get away and free me?"

"There were three of them at the house then. Caleb and the two big guys, Eric and Dale. I cooked a meal for them. Meatloaf. I make a great meatloaf. As they were eating, Caleb got a call and went to the backyard to take it. I pretended I was cleaning up the sink and slipped a knife out of the block and held it against my forearm. I said I needed to use the bathroom. One of the guys said he'd go with me, but the other one put his hand on his arm and shook his head. Meatloaf builds trust."

"A good thing it does," I said.

"So does flushing the toilet, which I remembered to do right after I left you."

"When did they find out I was gone?"

"Not for awhile," she said. "I made chocolate pudding for dessert. Then coffee. Caleb went down to check on you. He came back up screaming at Eric and Dale, who scrambled around like scared mice. He told them to take me downstairs and tie me up. Then he had them leave. He wished me luck. Can you—"

The words caught in her throat.

"We think he got scared of what the Eurasians would do to him," Agent Ramos said. "So he ran out."

"What will all this mean for Karen?" I said.

Agent Ramos said, "We can keep her off the witness list. We have enough to proceed against Caleb Morrison and Gus Deveroes."

Karen said, "And what will all this mean for Mike?"

Agent Ramos ran her finger along the edge of the table. "His situation is a little more precarious."

"Good word, *precarious*," I said. "From the Latin *precarious*, which means to ask for help through prayer because the situation isn't so great."

"Is there anything you don't know?" Agent Ramos said.

"I don't know how to keep my mouth shut," I said.

Karen said, "Do you mean the Eurasians might come after him?"

"It's a remote possibility," Agent Ramos said. "But I have a feeling Mr. Romeo can handle that eventuality."

Karen reached over and put her hand on mine. "Stay safe, Mike."

"That's my plan," I said. "And what will you do?"

She shook her head. "I really don't know. It's all so weird right now. I need time."

"We'll make sure you have it," Agent Ramos said.

"You've got what it takes to carry on," I said. "I've seen it in you."

"Really?" she said, looking at me like she wanted to believe it.

"Guaranteed," I said.

T hree weeks went by. I was back on my beach. Back in LA where I belong. What happens in Vegas you can have.

It was a cool afternoon and fog was settling on the Pacific. The only sound was the waves lapping the shore —the rhythm of nature from the heart of the sea. I put my hands behind my head and stretched out on the sand.

I was almost asleep when I heard the motorcycle. It got to the edge of the Paradise Cove parking lot, then shut off. My solitude would be coming to an end. But the beach is big and I was in a generous spirit now. My leg was almost a hundred percent and new hair had sprouted over the wound I'd picked up in the desert.

A voice said, "Just where you ought to be."

I sat up. "Noah! How ... where ..."

He sat on the sand. He was wearing boots, black jeans, and a black jacket. "Time enough for that."

"I thought they got you."

"They thought so, too. But I'm squirrelly. I escaped their Podunk jail. I got my bike back. And I know how to melt into the desert."

"How'd you find me?"

"You told me about this place, remember? Paradise Cove. What a name. I had to see it for myself. The fellow at the gate must have liked my face."

"What's not to like?" I said.

Noah smiled.

"Where's Bill?" I said.

Noah laughed. "Bill's still with Moochie. I found him there after all that carnage you unleashed. Boy, old Dillard is never going to be the same."

"Which is a good thing," I said.

"So after I spend a little time with you, I'm going back for Bill. We're gonna take a stab at coming back to the world."

"You sure?" I said.

"Light a candle instead of cursing the darkness," he said.

"I hope that still works."

"I know you believe it."

And maybe, at that moment, I did.

"How about something to eat?" I said. "I may have a can of pinto beans in my hut."

"Ah, just like back home," Noah said. "Let's eat."

AUTHOR'S NOTE

Many thanks for reading *Romeo's Stand*. I greatly appreciate it. Added appreciation would come if you would kindly leave a review on the Amazon site. For ebook readers, the link to do so is below (you may be asked to sign in to your Amazon account).

Leave a review for Romeo's Stand

The Romeo books can be read in any order, but if you'd like to know the order they were published, it is as follows:

1. Romeo's Rules
2. Romeo's Way
3. Romeo's Hammer
4. Romeo's Fight

MORE THRILLERS FROM JAMES SCOTT BELL

The Ty Buchanan Legal Thriller Series

#1 Try Dying
#2 Try Darkness
#3 Try Fear

"Part Michael Connelly and part Raymond Chandler, Bell has an excellent ear for dialogue and makes contemporary L.A. come alive. Deftly plotted, flawlessly executed, and compulsively readable. Bell takes his place as one of the top authors in the crowded suspense genre." - **Sheldon Siegel**, *New York Times* bestselling author

The Trials of Kit Shannon Historical Legal Thrillers

Book 1 - City of Angels
Book 2 - Angels Flight
Book 3 - Angel of Mercy
Book 4 - A Greater Glory
Book 5 - A Higher Justice

Book 6 - A Certain Truth

"With her shoulders squared and faith set high, Kit Shannon arrives in 1903 Los Angeles feeling a special calling to practice law ... Packed full of genuine, deep and real characters ... The tension and suspense are in overdrive ... A series that is timeless!" — **In the Library Review**

Stand Alone Thrillers

Your Son Is Alive
Blind Justice
Don't Leave Me
Final Witness
Framed

Mallory Caine, Zombie-At-Law Series

You read that right. A new genre. Part John Grisham, part Raymond Chandler—it's just that the lawyer is dead. Mallory Caine, Zombie at Law, defends the creatures no other lawyer will touch...and longs to reclaim her real life.

Pay Me In Flesh
The Year of Eating Dangerously
I Ate The Sheriff

ABOUT THE AUTHOR

 **James Scott Bell** is a best-selling author of thrillers and books on the writing craft. He is a winner of the International Thriller Writers Award and the Christy Award (Suspense). He studied writing with Raymond Carver, graduated with honors from USC Law School, and practiced law with a large litigation firm before beginning his writing career. He lives and writes in Los Angeles.

JamesScottBell.com

CPSIA information can be obtained
at www.ICGtesting.com
Printed in the USA
LVHW090550290820
664466LV00007B/1275

9 780910 355506